PAIGE AND THE RELUCTANT ARTIST

DARCI GARCIA

5 PRINCE PUBLISHING

Published by 5 PRINCE PUBLISHING & BOOKS, LLC

PO Box 865, Arvada, CO 80001

www.5PrinceBooks.com

ISBN digital: 978-1-63112-285-9

ISBN print: 978-1-63112-286-6

Cover Credit: Marianne Nowicki

Antonio Vicente Garcia, Sr. More of a father than a father-in-law, he was a constant source of encouragement and love. I will always remember him following my mother-in-law, Alice, in through the door as we celebrated every holiday and birthday in true Cuban style. In his hands was the inevitable tray of yucca, my favorite, with some extra for me to keep for later. He was a man of deep convictions, a man of character, a man of honor, a man who valued family above all else. I miss his laughter, his pep talks and his joy of life. But most of all, most of all, I miss his love. Until we meet again on that distant shore, this one is for you.

ACKNOWLEDGMENTS

Special thanks to my husband Tony who never stops cheering me from the sidelines. Also, my stepfather Raymond Martin for raising five hellion children with patience and grace, my most extraordinary friend Tracey for her years of friendship and love as well as her amazing mother, Hazel Gail Janas and lastly, my brothers Michael and Keith, who always knew I could.

PUBLISHER ACKNOWLEDGEMENTS

Thank you to Cate Byers, Marianne Nowicki, Bernadette Soehner, and Morgan Herrera for your assistance in the publication of Page and the Reluctant Artist by Darci Garcia.

ALSO BY DARCI GARCIA

Megan's Choice

Paige and the Reluctant Artist

PAIGE AND THE RELUCTANT ARTIST

CHAPTER 1

Paige Liston leaned against the black rental SUV, staring down at the broken heel of her Christian Louboutin shoe. Raising her head slightly, she scanned the desolate road behind her. Even the spectacular backdrop of rugged mountains; their jagged peaks reaching majestically towards a cloudless sky, failed to pull her from her wretched mood. With a sigh of frustration, she swiped a stray piece of blonde hair from her forehead before tucking it impatiently behind her ear. She had been driving this stretch of dirt road for forty minutes and had not yet seen another vehicle. Exhausted, Paige had thought to take a quick break to stretch her long legs. Instead, she had twisted her ankle stepping out of her vehicle. Mentally reprimanding people who insisted on living in the middle of nowhere, she climbed back into the SUV, taking off her other shoe first and throwing it onto the passenger seat. Paige again checked her phone and sighed when it showed there were still no bars.

"I have to be close," she muttered. Before she had lost signal, the GPS showed she had been within several miles of the Montana ranch that belonged to Mark Richards. Reaching into her makeup case, she pulled out a pale pink lipstick. Adjusting the rearview mirror, she applied it carefully, noting that her pale violet eyes were slightly bloodshot from the long plane ride. Smiling quickly to be sure none made it onto her perfect white teeth, she placed the lipstick back in the bag.

"You can do this," she stated firmly as she pulled back onto the road. "Just go in there, promise him the world, and he's yours." Turning up the stereo, Paige tried to calm her nerves. This was always the hardest part. Convincing an artist to sign with a gallery could be extraordinarily difficult, but signing on an unknown could be close to impossible.

MARK RICHARDS' ART PIECE HAD SURFACED SEVERAL MONTHS AGO while she had been attending a small gathering in Brooklyn. It was unusual for her to stray outside of Manhattan, although she had spent most of her childhood in the Bronx. Relentless, her friend Camilla had finally convinced her to go. It was there that Paige had first observed Mark Richards' work.

She had almost missed it completely. Placed on a small table in the entryway, it rested casually against dove-colored walls. It was simple yet arresting. The subject matter would have normally been underwhelming, a horse standing at the edge of a paddock, the backdrop a beautiful vista comprised of mountains and wildflowers. Yet this artist had done something remarkable. He had managed painting outwards, freeing the subject from the canvas. The colors, while mostly muted, drew the eye, pinning the observer's attention. The artist clearly wanted this stallion noticed above all else, and he succeeded. Entirely silver except for a small patch of white that only covered a quarter of his mane, he stood proudly, head raised so that you could see the corded muscles stretched beneath the sleek coat. His intense gaze was focused on something known only in the artist's imagination. Paige could almost feel the breeze that swayed the myriad wildflowers. The sky was slightly cloudy, yet the creation of shafts of sunlight saved it from being gloomy. Paige could almost hear the horse's breath blowing out softly through his gently flared nostrils, a sweet nickering of welcome. There was so much detail that she had picked up the canvas, the better to study it. She wanted to crawl inside and run her fingers down the stallion's thick neck. But what really took her breath away, elicited goose-bumps, made her heartbeat faster, were the stallion's eyes. When she searched them something inside her hurt, for in their depths she could see the suffering he had endured. Paige ran her fingers over the canvas as though to comfort him, pausing while she tried to compose herself. It was signed -*Mark Richards*-. She had never heard of him but nonetheless was determined that she would find him. It had taken Camilla coming to physically pull her out of the entryway for Paige to put the canvas down.

"What are you doing?" she asked, her brows furrowed in annoyance. "You have been standing here for ten minutes."

"It's my job, Camilla," she answered, still distracted by the canvas. Observing her friend's irritation, she sighed loudly. "Fine," she conceded reluctantly, placing the treasure back where she had found it. "But you do remember I'm an art curator, right?"

In fact, Paige Liston was one of the very best and in high demand among the New York gallery elites. Paige did not just love art. She absorbed it, breathing it in like oxygen. Her mother had shared once that her father, who had died when Paige was just two, had loved to paint, often working from used canvases thrown in the trash because they couldn't afford new ones. He had never believed that his art was anything special. One day her mother had given her the only painting she had kept, the rest discarded years before. Paige had wept when she held the small canvas, her tears rolling off onto the only tangible item she had from him. She remembered thinking how extraordinary, how brilliant his creation was as she held it in her trembling hands. He had died penniless, his greatest talent relegated to a dusty attic. At just twenty-six, a graduate of Pratt University, she was one of the youngest ever to have worked with the esteemed Paul Roja of Roja Galleries. Paige knew she came from the wrong side of the tracks. The Bronx did not mesh with the Manhattanites and Paige had always felt the sting of their rejection. Roja Galleries catered to very elite artists, those with a tremendous following, but too, sought those who had yet to be discovered. The rich and famous that she had once felt would be forever elusive now called her for help in procuring precious art from all over the world. Paul was now in his sixties, and Paige thought of him as a father.

It had been just her and her mother, Liane, until she, too, had passed away two years ago unexpectedly. It had taken Paige months to feel whole again, and Paul had been with her every step of the way, even bringing her favorite Thai food from the small restaurant around the corner from her uptown apartment. She had settled down a very long way from the poor neighborhood she had grown up in. Her mother had struggled to keep a roof over their heads, and Paige had hated to see her so exhausted. She remained determined that her parents' fate would not be her own. That another brilliant artist would never fall between the cracks because they were poor. Working hard had allowed her the life she thought she wanted, living in the classiest neighborhood, wearing the best designer clothing. She had carefully molded herself into someone that mattered.

"Well, it's not your painting, and this is a party," Camilla stated, forcing Paige back from her thoughts. "Can we please just mingle and have fun?"

Feeling guilty, she nodded, glancing over her shoulder longingly one more time before finally following her friend, who was already one cocktail ahead.

That night Paige had convinced the owner, the painter's aunt, to allow her to have Paul look at the piece. As she suspected, he thought it was extraordinary, reaching out himself to Mr.

Richards. It was after this conversation when Paul shared with Paige Mark's reluctance to share any of his work. Roja Gallery was known throughout the world. Artists represented in their Manhattan location were the very best and should your work be selected, you could consider yourself as having 'arrived' not only as an artist, but in New York's high society as well. Mr. Richards, however, did not live in New York. He lived in Helena, Montana.

"Where?" Paige asked, her face reflecting the horror at the prospect as Paul advised her where she would need to travel to meet the unwilling artist. "Isn't that just mountains minus civilization," she complained, appalled at the idea. Paige loved New York. The city was alive and vibrant, full of culture and romance and clothes and restaurants. It was an extraordinary mecca of diversions.

"Paul, seriously, do I really need to go all the way to, where is it again, Montana?"

"Helena," he replied dryly, unimpressed with Paige's theatrics.

"Yes, you need to go, and you will go."

PAIGE WAS SO PREOCCUPIED WITH HER MISERY THAT SHE ALMOST missed the small wooden sign that announced the entrance to Caramel Ranch. "Oh, thank Louis Vuitton," she muttered, relieved to have finally reached her destination. Stopping briefly on the dirt road leading to the ranch, she put the SUV into park and, reaching back, grabbed her Chanel duffle bag. Inside was a spare pair of shoes.

See? she thought, mentally applauding her foresight. *People think you're crazy for carrying spare shoes, but who's crazy now?* Taking them out, she quickly put them on, placing her other pair in the bag. She held the broken one against her chest for a few moments, mourning its loss before placing it in the bag as well. Taking a deep breath, she continued down the narrow dirt road. For the first thousand feet there were giant Quaking Aspens, enormous oxygen factories that stretched close to eighty feet. At their peak, they bowed to each other, kissing lightly. Lining both sides of the gravel drive, their canopy allowed the sun to rain effervescent droplets, enveloping Paige with the warmth of their welcome. Slowly, she opened her window, breathing in the earthy scents, its petrichor unfamiliar to her senses. Immediately she felt herself relax, as inhaling deeply, she continued slowly on. Paige found herself strangely unwilling to leave the comfort of the sheltering haven. However, her breath caught at the spectacular vista awaiting.

"Holy amazing mansion," she breathed out as the trees suddenly parted, opening to a wide circular drive. Mark Richards' home sat majestically in the middle of a vast oasis of green. All white, it was very much reminiscent of the Greek Revival mansions of the old south, complete with six large pillars. Paige fell instantly in love with the wide verandas running the full length of the home on both floors. Spectacular floor-to-ceiling windows covered the entire first floor of the home. Enormous blue antique double doors crooked their wooden fingers, inviting her in. Overflowing hanging plants hung above the porch rail, the colors a kaleidoscope encompassing a rainbow's spectrum. To the left, beneath a giant cedar tree, rested a double chaise, its plush pillows an exact color match to the door. The porch itself had several oversized rocking chairs, as well as a hammock with outdoor ceiling fans placed strategically above them all. As Paige pulled into the driveway, she noticed the stable towards the back of the home. A white fence that went too far back for Paige to see from her vantage point surrounded it. In the far distance, she could see horses standing quietly, at least four, from what she could tell. She had fully expected that Mark Richards lived a very humble existence, yet this was anything but humble. It was extraordinarily beautiful and modern, considering the location. Paige suddenly felt ashamed of her preconceived judgement. She was so busy looking at the property that she never noticed the man who was standing on the porch, his intense gaze following her as she exited the vehicle.

MARK RICHARDS WAS DREADING THIS VISIT, ONCE AGAIN regretting his decision. Paul Roja had been very convincing. While Mark had appreciated his direct approach, it was the fact that Mr. Roja had known of his parents' altruistic endeavors that had ultimately led him to consider his request. Despite Mark insisting he had no intention of selling his artwork, Mr. Roja had promised that if, after his curator's visit he still felt the same, he would never bother him again. Mark's impression was that had he not agreed, Mr. Roja might make a pest of himself. He had every intention of making this a brief visit, until, that is, he watched the blonde beauty make her way to the front of her truck. Mark felt the attraction like a punch to his gut. Tall, her blonde hair rested just below her waist. From his vantage point on the porch, he could make out full lips and even fuller breasts. Her white blouse was semi-sheer, hinting at the flesh that spilled provocatively from the top of her bra. He almost laughed when he observed her attempt to pull her heel out of the wet earth, a result of the rain that had soaked the ground last night. He wondered if Paul was banking on her beauty to get him to sign and smiled to himself at the thought. Mark was no stranger to the attentions of beautiful women. Beautiful women were every-where, but a woman with compassion, a woman who could see beyond the physical to the heart, still eluded him. He couldn't go anywhere without experiencing blatant interest; however, he was unmoved by the adulation. Mostly.

IT DIDN'T HURT THAT HE WAS EXTREMELY WEALTHY, HAVING inherited his trust fund at age twenty-three. His parents had perished in a plane crash on their way back from Africa. They were fervent animal rights activists trying to stop the senseless murders of elephants for their tusks. Mark had been just fifteen, and he still missed them both like it was yesterday. With no other living relatives, it was his maternal aunt who had stepped in and given Mark all the love that she could. It had been in her home that Ms. Liston had noticed his painting. After graduating from college with a degree in business, he had picked up where his parents had left off, but for Mark, his passion for saving animals had led him to horses. He had been on a trip to Montana, visiting his college friend Steve Carter, when he was first introduced to their plight. After Steve had picked him up from the airport, they had headed out on the long drive to his friend's home. He had been astonished by the wide-open spaces, the backdrop a rugged majestic landscape, its mountains proud and commanding. What had really sealed the deal however was the vast areas of verdant space. Mark loved New York but the only green space was in Central Park which he felt was always too crowded. He had never known how much, however, until his visit to this stunning oasis.

Mark observed the ample pastureland, remarking on the cattle and horses roaming freely. It was then that Steve had shared with him his sadness over the fate of old horses. He himself had saved several, however, his finances were not such that he could handle more than that. In fact, he planned on heading to the auction house where many of these poor creatures were being sold off. His passion for saving animals on high alert, Mark had joined him.

That was the day Mark was introduced to Storm Cloud. A stallion, his previous owner had used him first for racing then for stud. Now, he no longer served any purpose, so he was being discarded. Mark felt his rage rise, that any animal should be treated with so little regard. The two had approached the small makeshift corral and Mark had instantly been drawn to the stallion. He seemed to keep away from the other horses, standing proudly, an island unto himself. Mark made his way to where the animal stood. Just as he was about to reach out to touch him, he heard a voice behind him.

"I wouldn't do that if I were you," the stranger remarked. "Storm Cloud's as mean as they come. I should know. Been on the receiving end of his teeth and hooves a few times. I can't wait to get rid of him." Turning, Mark observed an older gentleman, maybe in his late sixties. He wore denim coveralls, his face weathered. He held his cowboy hat, tapping it on his leg as he looked over at his horse, not attempting to hide his dislike.

Without responding, Mark turned back, slowly reaching out his hand, running it gently down his flank. With a loud snort, the horse swung his head, looking directly into Mark's eyes. He knew that this proud beast was assessing him, so Mark held his gaze, his own eyes reflecting only compassion. In that moment he felt an instant connection, so visceral he could barely conceal the wave of emotion that threatened to overwhelm him, as he swallowed convulsively to mask the strength of his response.

"Well boy," he said. "It looks like it's you and me from now on." He had purchased Storm Cloud that day despite not yet having any way to care for him. Steve had kept him at his stable and within two weeks, Mark had purchased his own property. Since then, six other horses had joined Storm Cloud, the most recent purchased on his thirtieth birthday. Mark remained determined to save as many as he could.

CHAPTER 2

GRABBING HER PURSE OFF THE SEAT, PAIGE STEPPED OUT, slamming the door as she walked to the front of the SUV. The ground instantly sucked in one of her shoes. Cursing under her breath, she pulled it out, hearing a sucking sound as the mud finally released it. If Paige thought the home a surprise, then her first impression of Mark Richards was a bombshell.

That cannot be him, she thought, trying to school her features, positive that her jaw was somewhere on the soggy grass. *No way is that him.* Then, suddenly horrified, she wondered if he had heard her swearing. Paige had trouble taking all of Mark Richards in at once. His size was daunting. Standing at about six feet four, he was powerfully built with large muscular arms that were currently crossed in front of him. His jeans were well fitting, hugging his thick set legs, which were spread slightly apart. As she approached, he came down the steps until they were face to face. At almost five feet ten inches, there were very few people Paige had to look up to, but this man was one of them. Reaching out her hand, she looked into his eyes, the color of a thundercloud wrapped in lightning. They stared out of a perfectly chiseled face that was cleanly shaven. His hair was obsidian, with maybe just a few fireworks thrown in. *He's almost too much of a man*, she thought abstractly. He was beautiful. She smiled widely and wondered if her lipstick had made it to her teeth again.

Damn, why didn't you check one more time? she lamented. Mark smiled back, but his manner was reserved. *He's going to take some convincing*, she thought.

"Hello Mr. Richards," she said breathlessly, wondering what the hell had happened to her voice which sounded like she had just run a marathon, which was highly unlikely since she hated all forms of exercise. "I'm Paige Liston. Your home is simply stunning," she remarked as she spread her arm out expansively, hitting him in the chest. "Oh, I'm sorry," she apologized, putting her arm back down. "It's just so, so—"

"Yes, beautiful. I know," he responded dryly. "Call me Mark," he said, turning on his heel. Speaking over his shoulder, he asked, "Would you like a drink? I have water, lemonade and beer."

"Oh no, I'm fine," she replied, falling into step beside him. He didn't speak again as Paige followed him through the door into the foyer. She sucked in her breath slowly through her teeth, amazed at the spectacular scene before her. Paige could see all the way to the other side of the home where floor to ceiling windows brought the beautiful landscape indoors. To either side of her, twin curved staircases rose majestically to the space above. Straight ahead, to the left, the room branched off to the gourmet kitchen. She guessed the ceilings to be at least twenty feet high. The island alone had seating for ten, the antique blue cabinets rising above countertops of sea gray and white. The tone was masculine and homey, inviting all who entered to sit and relax. To the right was a vast living area with a whitewashed fireplace that encompassed an entire wall, its mantel constructed entirely of driftwood. There were two wide hallways, one to the right of the kitchen, the other to the left of the living room. Paige assumed there were bathrooms and guest rooms galore. Mark led her to a large, navy Chesterfield sofa that wrapped comfortably around an enormous driftwood table. Two matching overstuffed chairs flanked the sofa, all strategically placed so that you might not only enjoy the fireplace on a cold winter's evening, but you would never lose sight of the glorious landscape. Lovely side chairs, placed thoughtfully, gave it the same welcoming feel. She sat facing the large windows, enjoying the stunning view. Pastureland seemed to go on for miles. Here and there, Paige could see two or three beautifully sculpted flower gardens. She did not know what types of flowers there were, but the effect was breathtaking. The white fence weaved in and out of the garden areas and it was then that Paige noticed even more horses, along with another stable, each appearing to hold approximately thirty stalls. The property extended much further than she had imagined.

Suddenly, just off to the left, she caught a flash of silver and then he was there. The stallion. The one from the canvas. Even from this distance, Paige could see how much more he was. Not even Mark's extraordinary talent could capture the incredible spirit of this beast. Standing, Paige walked to the window, staring out, at once enraptured by his beauty. Without thinking, she placed her hand on the glass as if to reach out and touch him. She had to see him face to face. Almost as though he knew he was being observed, the beautiful creature raised his head. He appeared to be looking directly at her. Paige could see the flash of white on his mane, the exemplary lines of muscle rippling under his shiny coat. *Hammered silver*, she thought. Paige was so mesmerized that she didn't realize Mark was standing beside her until he spoke.

"He's incredible, isn't he?" Looking up, Paige could see the love he had for this creature. It was palpable, emanating from him.

"What's his name?" she asked, her focus once again on the beautiful beast.

"Storm Cloud," he replied, as he turned. With a last worshipping glance, Paige followed, sitting across from him, wondering why the scent of his cologne made her want to lick him. *Great way to keep it professional,* she silently reprimanded herself.

"I can see why you bought him," she said, tossing her best smile.

"I rescued him," he stated dryly. "His owner was going to put him down."

Her expression horrified, Paige responded, her voice incredulous.

"Put him down? But why? I mean he's stunning,"

"He's old," Mark said, shaking his head. "He was a champion, but he suffered an injury that he couldn't come back from. They tried putting him out to stud, but he was a handful. They had him in a stall by himself, no interaction with anyone except the old man they hired to feed him." Paige could see the anger on Mark's face.

"They maltreated him, so I offered to buy him, and the rest, as they say, is history."

"Do you do that often?" Paige asked, her expression curious.

"Do what?"

"Rescue horses. It sounds like he might not have been your first one."

With a slight smile, Mark nodded.

"He was my first, but certainly not my last. I cannot stand by and see any animal hurt or abused. It is why I moved here. I needed the land, and that wasn't happening in New York."

"New York," she exclaimed, sitting forward. "You used to live there?"

Nodding, Mark continued. "Yes, for several years after my parents were killed in a plane crash."

"Oh, I'm so sorry," Paige said, her expression sympathetic. "I lost both my parents as well."

Mark studied the woman before him. He had to admit that up

close she was even more beautiful; her features perfectly placed, her lips not too full, but it was her eyes that most captivated him. Facing her by the window, he had been momentarily startled by their incredible hue, the color reminiscent of what one might expect to see were you hold a violet up to the sun. There were soft freckles that played lightly over her cheeks, though he sensed she tried to hide them. Mark found himself liking her, even aside from the physical. There was just something about her, something just below the surface that he couldn't quite put his finger on.

Still, he wasn't doing an art show. No way.

"Ms. Liston," he began.

"Oh, please just call me Paige," she hurriedly interrupted. "No need for formalities."

Clearing his throat Mark continued.

"Yes, well, Paige. I think I should tell you right now that I have no interest in doing a show. My art isn't for sale. I do it strictly for pleasure as I repeatedly mentioned to Mr. Roja."

"Oh, I see," she replied, a look of disappointment crossing her features. "I could guarantee you a great deal of money, Mark. I don't think you realize just what you would be passing up."

"I don't need the money. Not to be crude but my parents were extremely wealthy and now, so am I. Again," he continued, his voice resolute. "I do my art for pleasure, a way to unwind. I certainly never believed it to be anything special. I'm afraid you have wasted your time coming here."

"Yes, Paul said as much," she replied, her expression contemplative. Standing, she walked once more to the large window. Storm Cloud was still there, his piercing gaze moving swiftly through her. *Think, Paige. Think*, she commanded herself. Then like the proverbial lightbulb going off she had it. *Fingers crossed*, she thought.

"Mark, I have a proposition," Paige began, her eyes never leaving the horse. "I think you might just like it."

Rising, he crossed the room, once again standing beside her, his hands resting casually in his pants pockets. Cocking his head to one side, he said.

"I'm listening."

Taking a deep breath, she plunged in.

"If you agree to just one show, ten pieces of art, anything you want to paint, the subject completely at your discretion, we will donate one million dollars to the rescue of your choice, either here in the United States or elsewhere. Any organization you choose."

Turning, she met his eyes. "I know you're rich, Mark, but even you must admit that a million dollars could save a great many animals."

The offer was both a surprise and outrageous. Frankly, he was astounded. He knew virtually nothing of the world of art. However, that amount was much more than he had ever imagined.

"Well?" Paige asked. "Do we have a deal?"

Shaking his head, Mark said, "I need to think about it. Ten pieces will take time and right now I'm handling much of the care of the animals myself. I will need to get help here before I can begin."

"No problem," Paige replied, her tone brisk. "Hire anyone you need and send us the bill."

"Well, it's not quite that easy," Mark explained. "Not everyone can care for horses. I will need to find experienced hands. I will require assistance here in the house as well. I have been meaning to hire a caretaker, but I've been very busy. It has twenty-three rooms," he finished, opening his arms widely. "It will probably require several people to run if I have to paint most days."

"Got it handled," Paige responded, sensing victory was imminent. "I will personally see that all the help you need is hired immediately."

"You sound pretty confident," Mark said, his expression

amused. "I can see now why Paul sent you. You don't like being told no, do you?"

Smiling, Paige shrugged.

"I just know what I want, and I want you."

Raising his eyebrows, Page quickly explained. "I mean to paint. I want you to paint," Paige repeated, clearly flustered.

"Oh," Mark replied, his voice laced with disappointment. "So, it's just my painting you want? Because I could certainly make the rest of me available as well."

Blushing furiously, Paige refused to respond. Instead, she grabbed her purse from the couch and headed towards the doors, shoulders stiff. She attempted to fling the door open dramatically but it was so heavy that she barely managed to open it at all, despite pulling with all her body weight. As she made her way to her vehicle, Mark tried not to laugh when her heels got stuck once again, requiring her to stop, yanking them several times to release them. She didn't say a word until she stood by her truck door. Opening it, she threw her purse onto the passenger side seat. Tossing an angry glare towards Mark, she spoke.

"Let me be perfectly clear, Mr. Richards," she spat out. "I am a professional. I take tremendous pride in what I do. I am educated, intelligent and generally, an amiable person. That I am also a woman is moot. I am not now, nor will I ever be available to entertain you in any way other than providing a business dinner or two. Do you understand me?" she finished, her ample chest heaving below a face that was currently a beautiful shade of bright pink.

Mark realized immediately that this woman was different. He also knew that his instinct about her had been correct. There was much more to Paige than he realized. He hadn't meant to be insulting to her, yet he would be lying if he said there wasn't a part of him that wanted to know just how far she would go to get his artwork. Observing her now, face flushed, eyes narrowed in anger, slim shoulders pulled back, he felt his attraction to her like a visceral pull. He wanted her. Not just sexually, although right now, with her ample breasts pressed against her sheer top, it was hard to not want to dive into her, but on a deeper level. First, though, he needed to apologize, and quickly.

Paige watched as Mark made his way towards her, drawing in her breath sharply as she noted how his muscular legs ate the ground, his expression covered in raw determination. Her attraction to this man was unlike anything she had ever felt before. It was something wild, untethered, relentlessly pulsing through her. It left her feeling vulnerable and confused. *He scares me*, she thought, shocked by the realization. But why? Then he was standing before her. Looking up, her breath caught at the kindness in his eyes.

"I apologize, Paige," Mark stated, his voice contrite. "It was a crude comment, one for which I have no excuse. If we could just start over?"

Paige, sensing he was sincere, felt herself relax. Nodding, she turned and climbed into the SUV. Her hand on the door, she replied.

"Apology accepted. I'm excited to be working with you, Mark. I genuinely mean that. You have an extraordinary gift, a very rare gift." Closing her door, she slid the window down.

"I will be in touch soon about the help that you will need. I may need to fly back again but I will go over that with you later."

A picture of Paige lying naked on his bed suddenly flashed through Mark's mind. He felt his physical response slam into him. He quickly spun away as, speaking over his shoulder, he assured her she would be welcome at any time. Her expression perplexed at his sudden departure, Paige slowly drove away. She could see Mark leaning against a pillar in her rearview mirror and wondered how on earth she was going to keep her attraction to him hidden. Every part of her was on fire, but she never mixed business with pleasure. It was a hard rule, one that she had broken once and was still suffering the consequences for.

Her mind went back to another man, another artist, who had temporarily won her heart until he had shown her, he had none. It had been a brutal breakup; he had been angry and ugly towards her for a very long time. Paige remembered it as though it were yesterday, though it had been two years since they had been a couple. She still avoided him at all costs, although they ran in the same circles, so to speak. Kyle Pratt was a dangerous man, one that Paige never wanted to see again. While she didn't know Mark Richards yet, she remained determined to keep him at arm's length. She didn't trust herself and what she felt for him already told her he, too, was a dangerous man, although unlike Kyle, Mark could potentially claim her heart. She accepted then why she had felt the fear. *No*, she thought, determination foremost in her mind. *It will be strictly business with Mark.* Feeling better, Paige flew home the next day, ready to do the work she felt compelled to do; bring beauty to the world.

CHAPTER 3

Exhausted from her trip, Paige sat with her feet resting on the coffee table, staring out at the New York skyline. She considered how flat it appeared compared to the mountainous landscape she had just visited, which, surprisingly, she found herself missing. *Ridiculous*, she told herself. *They're mountains. Just take a rustic vacation and get it out of your system.* Her cat, Chloe, lay across her lap, purring contentedly as Paige stroked her soft fur gently. She could not get Mark out of her head.

Paul had been overjoyed by the deal, although he had gone several shades of white when Paige mentioned what it would cost them. It was an exorbitant amount to pay an unknown, but they both knew that this man had a rare talent. They would make their money back three-fold. Upon arriving back home she had made all the arrangements for the help that Mark would need, and he had called her last night to advise her he had hired several of the applicants already.

His voice had sent a frisson of excitement through her, which she promptly squashed. "He's a client, he's a client, he's a client," she repeated to herself. No matter what, Paige remained unwavering that their relationship remain business only.

Hearing the front door open, Paige smiled as she observed her friend place her Chanel purse on the granite countertop. Camilla Spears was the exact opposite to Paige. She was exotic in every way. Her kohl black hair was voluminous, with a natural glossy wave that she did nothing to quell. It was down now, resting just below the nape of her swan-like neck. Her figure was svelte but not overly thin and they both complained often about the size of their breasts, finding them too large at times. Tossing her jacket carelessly over the kitchen chair, Camilla slid out of her shoes as she made herself comfortable in the camel club chair, directly across from its larger mate. Chloe instantly jumped from Paige's lap, quickly making her way to Camilla. With a short laugh, Paige pointed at her errant feline.

"Should I be jealous? Clearly, she hasn't missed me too much!"

Smiling down, Camilla shifted slightly to accommodate Chloe.

"No worries. You're still her momma. My pants are just softer," she finished, as she took over the task of petting her step-kitty.

"Would you like something to drink?" Paige asked, rising.

"No, I'm good. What I'm dying to know is how it went with your cowboy."

"Cowboy? Oh, you mean Mark Richards?"

"Yes, the artist from—where does he live, again?"

"Montana," Paige responded, laughing. "And he isn't a cowboy, for goodness' sake. He lived in New York most of his life."

"He did?" Camilla replied, eyes widened in surprise.

"Yes, he did. He only moved to Montana because he started a rescue for horses, and I guess that's where he could find the most land."

"Oooooh," Camilla replied, her expression inquisitive. "Horses? How odd."

"So, what's he like? Young or old?"

"Our age, I think," Paige replied thoughtfully. "I don't know exactly, though. But he was nice and of course the most important thing is; he agreed to do ten pieces," she finished, gleefully clapping her hands.

"Of course he did," Camilla replied, amused. "How could any man refuse you?"

Shaking her head, Paige chuckled.

"No, it wasn't that. He may just be better looking than any man I have ever met."

"Oh, wait a minute!" Camilla exclaimed, coming forward in her chair, spilling Chloe to the floor. "Do tell! And I mean everything!"

Laughing, Paige went on to give Camilla the details of her visit. Yet, even while she spoke, there was an underlying restlessness whenever her mind brought up his image. It was a decidedly uncomfortable, as well as alien sensation.

Camilla appeared completely engrossed by the details and Paige marveled at her friend's inner beauty, which was rivaled only by her outer beauty. They had both met at college during their freshman year. Paige remembered the first time she had seen Camilla, her long strides eating up the sidewalk leading from her sorority to the main campus. Stunning didn't quite capture Camilla. She exuded confidence, along with a mischievous nature that always erupted from her turquoise eyes. However, it was her kindness that had forged their friendship.

Paige had just lost her mother and was having a tough day, the kind where just everything goes wrong. She was late on her rent, late for her second job as a server at an exclusive uptown eatery, and as she stood on the steps of the university in the pouring rain, her favorite pink and white polka dot umbrella still on the subway where she had accidentally left it, she realized that her paper, overdue, was sitting on her kitchen table. Her professor had already given her one extension. Paige knew there wouldn't be another.

Suddenly, it was all too much. She couldn't call her best friend because that had been her mother. There wasn't anyone else close in her life, so everything was just pouring down on her like the beads of water that were whipping against her face, tiny liquid pellets of yet more pain. Head bowed; she felt a gentle hand on her shoulder. Without saying a word, the beautiful stranger had guided her indoors to the ladies' room. She had given her paper towels to dry her face after which she had enfolded her in a much-needed hug. Paige had then proceeded to let go of the rest of her pent-up tears. They had been friends ever since. The recipient of a very substantial trust fund from her grandmother, Camilla could have chosen to live the life of luxury, yet instead had obtained a degree in psychology. Finishing her Masters, she now worked for a nonprofit that offered free counseling to the homeless. It was brutal, heartbreaking work, yet Camilla showed up every day, smiling that beautiful smile, ready to do what she could. She had purchased an apartment in the Bronx, rarely splurging on luxuries, although, glancing over at the Chanel bag resting on the kitchen counter, Paige wondered if maybe she had finally decided to treat herself. Seeing the direction of her gaze, Camilla spoke.

"Gorgeous, isn't it? My parents bought it for my birthday last year and I just found it the other day when I was cleaning out my closet."

Shaking her head, Paige laughed. "Of course you did! I should have known it had to be a gift. You never buy yourself anything extravagant."

Shrugging, a small smile playing against her lips, Camilla sighed.

"I know, I know. It's just… there is so much need, and, well—"

Glancing around her apartment, Paige felt a twinge of guilt. She had opted for an expensive uptown apartment with a view. It cost an exorbitant amount of money each month, more than she had ever believed she could afford. Yet, after graduating she had marched into the most exclusive gallery in New York City, demanded to see Paul Roja himself and had effectively landed the most sought-after position in any gallery. Thinking back to that day, Paige had felt her mother with her every step of the way, guiding and encouraging her. At least that's what Paige believed, and the thought brought her comfort.

Now, three years later, she was a force in her own right, gaining not only the respect of her friend and mentor Paul, but of the art community as well. If Paige said an artist was going to be big, they always were. And Paige believed that Mark Richards, rescuer of horses, would be the biggest yet. Her success had brought her financial stability as well. Her commissions well exceeded her salary and alone had netted her first million in earnings.

Unlike Camilla, Paige wanted it all, or so she had thought. Lately, though, the things she had amassed had brought her little joy. She felt a disquietude, a distinct sense that there was something more, something just out of reach that would perhaps be more fulfilling. Frustrated, it still eluded her.

Hearing her phone, Paige was pulled from her thoughts. When she saw it was Mark, she felt her heart begin to race. She quickly answered, mouthing an apology in Camilla's direction. Waving her on, Camilla scooped Chloe off the floor, then watched with amusement as she spun three times before finally settling back onto her lap.

"Hi Mark," Paige answered, hating the slightly breathless note in her voice. "I wasn't expecting to hear from you again so soon."

Mark's voice came back, deep, rich and altogether too sexy.

"Hi Paige. Listen, I apologize for bothering you, however, I wanted to thank you personally for the referrals. As you know I've hired most of the applicants, so I was able to start this morning on the first piece."

"Oh Mark! Really?" excitement evident in her voice. Paige felt the familiar rush of adrenaline she experienced whenever a new artist began to create. It was like she had discovered a great secret, one that would change the world, and it belonged to her. It was a crazy thought, but Paige genuinely invested herself in the entire artistic process.

Chuckling, Mark spoke.

"Yes, really. I just want to get through the pieces so I can get back to my real life. The sooner the better," he finished, his voice determined.

Feeling a quick stab of disappointment, Paige was reminded that Mark was not her typical artist. He was a reluctant one, and if she were honest, these were new waters she was treading. For the first time, Paige felt a twinge of uncertainty. The fact that he lived so far away didn't help. She was used to being able to visit her artists often, a kind of encouragement as well as the ability to watch the work unfold. But with Mark, that would be difficult, unless—

"Anyway," Mark continued, ignoring her silence, "I thought you should know."

"Yes, yes of course, Mark. I'm sorry, I was just thinking that perhaps, since you have started so quickly, I might find a place nearby to stay? Just for a few months?"

"Stay?" he asked, clearly confused.

Clearing her throat, Paige explained.

"Yes. I find that being close to the artists during their process helps. That way I can be available should you want me—or I'm sorry, I mean need me. Well, I'm sure you know what I mean," she finished, her complexion turning a deep red. Waiting for his response, Paige felt like an awkward teenager. She hated the feeling.

"Well, I don't know what you generally provide to your artists, however, I can assure you that I don't want or need anything. However, if it would make your process easier," he continued, "you are, of course, welcome to stay here. The house is large enough, as you know, so it would make no sense for you to stay elsewhere. Besides, there isn't a place to stay within two hours of here."

Glancing over at Camilla, she noted the surprised look on her friend's face, her eyes as wide as saucers.

"Well, let me think about it, Mark, and I do appreciate the offer. I'm glad you have the help you need, and I certainly look forward to working with you."

"Sure thing," he replied. "Have a good day. Talk to you soon."

After disconnecting, she looked back over at Camilla. Her expression was both curious as well as suspicious.

"You're going to stay there?" she cried, her expression incredulous. "There? In the woods, or the meadows," she squealed, waving her arms dramatically.

Shaking her head, Paige shrugged.

"Well, I have a lot at stake with this one," she explained, trying to hide the excitement she felt at being in such close proximity to Mark. "I mean, a million isn't chump change, and it's really more me keeping an eye on my—I mean on the gallery's investment," she corrected.

Crossing her arms, Camilla sat further back into the chair.

"I don't buy it," she stated, her tone disbelieving, "there is no way you would pack up for several months just to keep an eye on the gallery's investment. What's really going on?" she continued, tilting her head slightly. "There's something. I just know it."

With a frustrated groan, Paige answered.

"Ok, the truth is I was really attracted to him, like hard."

"So, what's wrong with that?" Camilla asked, confusion clear in her voice.

"Normally, nothing," Paige replied. "But he is a client, and I will not become romantically involved with a client. Not ever again."

"Ah, so that's it," Camilla replied, her tone sympathetic. "I get it." She knew what had happened in Paige's previous relationship and that she was still suffering the consequences of that decision.

"But if you feel such a strong attraction, then why place your-self literally onto his doorstep? That seems like a temptation you could avoid."

"I know," Paige returned. "It sounds like the definition of crazy, but," shrugging her shoulders, "I really feel it would be best for Paul and the gallery. I need to get over myself and do my job." Glancing down at Chloe, a concerned expression crossed Paige's features.

"I can't leave her for that long though." Holding up her hand to interrupt what she knew her friend would say, she continued. "No, you are not going to care for her for that length of time. I'll just have to take her with me."

"Um, shouldn't you check with Mark first?" Camilla asked, irritation at being interrupted before she could speak evident in her tone.

"It shouldn't be a problem. His home is massive and there weren't any dogs that I noticed."

Shrugging, Camilla spoke.

"Ok, but if he says no, you know I will do it. Besides," she continued, leaning forward to rub Chloe's head, "I think she likes me better anyway."

Laughing, Paige shook her head.

"Probably," she agreed. "She's nothing if not fickle."

Long after Camilla had gone, Paige still could not get Mark out of her thoughts. It was as though there were some unknown force driving her emotions. Paige had always prided herself on her ability to control her feelings. Certainly, she had learned her lesson in her previous relationship about wearing her heart on her sleeve. These days, she kept it wrapped tightly, completely out of view. She simply never wanted to endure the humiliation that she had suffered since her last breakup.

Paige hadn't mentioned it to Camilla, but Kyle had been calling her. The first time his name had come up on her caller ID, her heart had slammed into her throat. She had no intention of answering; ever, however, she couldn't help but wonder why he was trying to reach her. It was unsettling, especially remembering the last conversation they had ever had.

She had gone to his home, every inch of her finished with his special brand of abuse. Paige could still see him clearly. He always entered a room as if to say to everyone present, 'here I am', his expression slightly pinched, although his chiseled good looks hid most of the disdain he truly felt for those he considered to be beneath him. He had, as usual, been dressed in the latest fashion, manicured nails, hair perfectly tousled. Paige had been spellbound when she had first met him, losing herself completely in the notion that someone like him, wealthy, talented, the world at his feet, could possibly love someone like her. The girl from the wrong side of the tracks who wore off the rack clothing, wasn't sure which fork to use, and certainly had never dined in any of his favorite restaurants.

On that day, he had stood before her, his expression full of contempt. Kyle had never been able to reconcile that it had been her that had ended the relationship. His utter astonishment when Paige had finally worked up the courage to tell him exactly what she thought of him had been almost comical. She had observed his face as the flush of red traveled from his perfectly shaven, soft chest to his smooth-as-a-baby-butt face, the fury in his eyes sending her reeling backwards.

"Who do you think you are?" he had spat at her, jabbing his finger violently towards her, "to leave me? You were nothing when I met you and you are still nothing," he had finished, his lips pulled back in a sneer. Then he had cast his eyes slowly down her body, his thinly veiled disgust hitting every part of her like a fist, until finally, he had met her eyes. "You will come running back and I might even consider it," he stated, emitting a short bark of laughter, "if you can convince me that there is anything you have that I could possibly ever want again. I doubt it," he had finished, crossing his arms, his expression bitter. Paige had been trembling, frightened by the rage that was emanating from him. She had genuinely feared that he might even harm her, such was the power of his outrage. Bile rose up so that she thought she would be violently ill. Still, she had stood up to him.

"I can assure you, Kyle, that I will never want you back. Not today, not tomorrow. Not ever." Then she had walked, shoulders back, out of his apartment, the venom in his gaze striking squarely between her shoulder blades.

Six months later he suddenly approached her at the gallery. His appearance did nothing to her senses, except cause a shudder to run along her spine. For a moment she had again experienced a sudden bout of nausea, though thankfully it had passed quickly. He had been contrite, apologetic, almost humble though it all came off as wholly insincere. Kyle loved himself too much to be humble. He had wanted to ask her to come back; had stated that he was a changed man, that he missed her. It had been bizarre, given his final parting words which Paige knew were his true feelings. Still, she had tried to be kind when she once again made it clear that they had no future together. Ever. His parting look had been once again filled with bitterness as he spun on his heel, stalking out of the gallery, rage evident in his every movement.

That had been the last time she had spoken to him, although they had seen each other from time to time at various gallery openings. Always, he would tear her clothes from her violently with his gaze, his eyes filled with loathing. Paige could feel her body react to the memory and fought to control her rapid breathing. Lost in her thoughts she had not realized how high her level of anxiety had risen. She drew in a shuddery breath, allowing her body to relax. Kyle was out of her life now. Well, to a degree. He managed to make his presence known. Glancing at her phone she considered once again blocking his number, but he was a client with her gallery, although he had been instructed by Paul to only do business directly with him. Paul had been worried about Kyle's behavior and had wanted to dismiss him as a client.

"Paul, please don't," she had pleaded with him. "This was my fault. It was poor judgement on my part, and I don't want either you or the gallery to suffer financially as a result." It had been humiliating to hear the things that Kyle was spewing to others about her, but Paige had been determined that she suffer the consequences alone. Paul had finally agreed, albeit reluctantly. Deep down, Paige had held some hope that Kyle would leave on his own. Any gallery in New York would have gladly taken him, yet he had remained. It was why Paige would never allow herself to become involved with another client. That thought suddenly brought back the image of Mark. Shaking her head, Paige again wondered how she was ever going to deny her attraction for him, but she was determined to do so. She had to protect her heart. She had to.

CHAPTER 4

MARK HAD AGREED TO ALLOW PAIGE TO BRING CHLOE ALONG since she would be staying for an indeterminate amount of time. Thankfully, Chloe had remained quiet during the flight. As Paige made her way back to Mark's home on the now familiar stretch of highway, she glanced back in her rearview mirror to check on her. Chloe appeared completely unaffected, lying on her side in her plush carrier, leisurely licking her feet. Blinking her outrageously emerald eyes, she proceeded to curl up, no doubt to take one of her many long naps.

Smiling, Paige once again turned her attention ahead to the road, trying to ignore the plethora of butterflies winging their way through her stomach. She tried to tell herself it was just nerves, being in new surroundings, away from her comfort zone, however, deep down Page recognized it had little to do with her destination and everything to do with the man she would see there.

Mark had not been far from her thoughts. In fact, Paige had found it difficult to go through a day without pulling him up in her mind's eye. It had taken several weeks to button down all her current obligations as she prepared for the trip. Packing had been difficult since Paige dressed in all the latest fashion trends, so finding leisurely outfits appropriate for her surroundings had resulted in a great deal of frustration. She had finally gone shopping, purchasing several pairs of jeans, shorts, and casual tops. Mindful that the summers were short, she also included sweaters and heavier garments. All told, she had filled four large suitcases. It had cost her a bundle to check them, and she had required assistance to get them from gate to gate. It had been a logistical nightmare, especially with the added stress of carrying Chloe everywhere. She was grateful that Mark would be there to help her unload. An image of his broad shoulders and muscular arms hit her like a sharp jab to the gut just as she pulled off onto the long driveway. She again felt the welcome of the majestic trees that swayed gently above, their canopy welcoming her home. Shaking her head at the nonsensical thought, Paige caught her breath as she observed Mark standing on the front porch, his hands resting in his pants pockets.

He looks like every cowboy cliche ever, she thought. *Only better.* His blue jeans were faded, the fabric barely enough to contain the powerfully muscular thighs that pressed against them. His camel shirt was unbuttoned just enough that Paige could see the dark chest hair that peeked out, a temptation on its own. He had rolled the sleeves up, his muscled forearms flexing as he made his way down the steps.

She couldn't help but be reminded of Kyle's perfectly smooth, hairless chest. *Mark's is so much more primitive,* she thought, *so much sexier.* Paige was grateful for her sunglasses. She didn't trust her eyes not to reveal too much of what she was feeling. The last thing she wanted was for Mark Richards to know how forceful her attraction to him really was. Taking a deep breath, Paige opened the door, crossing her fingers that she would follow through on her promise to keep their relationship strictly business. Stepping out of the vehicle, she watched as Mark made his way to her, his stride confident, his masculinity a quiet roar. As he came to a stop, Paige realized that the promise to maintain her distance was going to be the hardest one she would ever keep. He was a force. A hurricane of pure maleness and Paige knew, like it or not, that she had just jumped into the eye of the storm.

MARK TRIED TO APPEAR CASUAL AS HE WATCHED PAIGE'S VEHICLE approach. He had taken longer than usual trying to decide what to wear, telling himself that she was a professional and deserved to at least find him showered and neat. He had been restless for several days now, and he didn't like it. After her departure, Mark had tried to shake off her effect on him. Usually, his horses and work on the ranch were enough to keep him occupied. He spent many hours working and exercising them, no small feat since at last count he had ten, but lately he had been feeling somewhat off. Like he was missing something.

If he were completely honest, Paige was the first woman since his mother, who had managed to take him down a few pegs. Her rebuff of his less-than-gentlemanly proposition had surprised him. Women didn't say no to Mark. Most knew that he was wealthy and being good looking didn't hurt either. But Mark wanted more. He wanted forever. Someone who didn't care about the money, or things that could be bought. His parents had been in love, devoted completely one to the other. It was this that Mark sought. That kind of visceral connection. Seeing the satisfaction his parents had rescuing animals and then his own experiences caring for those poor creatures that were disposed of once they no longer made money for their owners had opened a piece of his heart that he had never known existed. The truth was, he hadn't saved them, they had saved him.

As he approached Paige, it struck him that she appeared much different than she had the first time he had seen her. Then she had been wearing heels and an expensive outfit. Being raised in

New York, Mark knew something about fashion. Today, however, she was dressed casually. Her long-sleeved white button-down shirt was tucked loosely into a pair of dark denim jeans that hugged her slim hips. A plain black belt accentuated her tiny waist. A quick glance at her feet prompted a smile. She had traded in the heels for sneakers. Her long hair was pulled back in a simple ponytail, stray pieces floating gently against makeup-free skin. Her freckles were much more prominent, and Mark still found them sexy as hell. She was so much more than beautiful and suddenly his hands began to sweat, something he hadn't experienced since his days in high school. She was captivating. Alluring. Mark was aware that this was to be a professional relationship. Something told him Paige was no pushover and frankly, he didn't want a relationship right now. He couldn't handle a repeat of his last relationship disaster. He was busy enough with the ranch along with the added responsibility of painting ten pieces, one of which was almost completed. Still, she did something to him, unsettled him, like an itch he couldn't quite reach. Determined to ignore these confusing emotions, he reached for her hand, shaking it much too heartily, then dropped it quickly, feeling a sudden flush rise to his face. Embarrassed, he spoke gruffly, trying to hide the fact that he felt like a damn schoolboy in her presence.

"I see you made it in one piece," he barked loudly. Startled, Paige flinched. Nodding, she turned, opening the back door to get Chloe. Speaking over her shoulder, she answered, her voice breathless because he did that to her.

"Yes, thankfully it was an uneventful trip."

Backing out, she stood too soon, hitting her head hard on the roof. Crying out loudly, she dropped the carrier back onto the seat, rubbing her head vigorously. Chloe, who, up to this point had been an absolute angel, began to howl like the demons from hell, causing Paige to once again grab the carrier. Turning quickly, she swung Chloe's carrier straight into Mark's chest, causing him to stumble back, then, horrifyingly, fall. Silence reigned for several humiliating seconds. Paige could hear the breeze moving along the treetops, birds singing, her heart pumping her blood at an alarming rate, and Chloe still howling in earnest. The spell broken, Mark stood quickly, brushing the dirt and gravel from his pants.

"I'm so terribly sorry," Paige began, pointing towards her errant cat as an excuse for her blunder.

"It was an accident," he said, staring inside the carrier at Chloe, a look of both fear and concern crossing his features. "Does she do that all the time?" he asked as they began walking towards the house.

"Oh, no, not at all. I think she's just tired from the trip. Really, she's normally very quiet." Appearing unconvinced, Mark reached for the front door handle when it suddenly swung open.

Mrs. Castillo was a petite woman in her fifties. Mark had hired her as the main housekeeper, charging her with procuring the rest of the household help as well as managing the day-to-day operations. Her curly hair reminded Paige of cotton balls; lovely, billowy and very white. It seemed to run amok, spinning off in different directions, yet the chaotic effect was endearing. Dressed in a crisp blue dress with a starched white apron over it, she was the epitome of a professional housekeeper, right down to her sensible white running sneakers. Paige liked her immediately. What stood out the most, however, was her brilliant smile.

"Hello," she trilled, excitement clear in her voice. "You must be Paige. My name is Maria. Mrs. Castillo is simply too formal," she said. "Mark has told me all about you. Come in, come in," she sang as she waved them through. Closing the door, she observed Paige's carrier. Glancing inside, she beamed. "Well, isn't she beautiful?" she exclaimed, her eyes lit with excitement. "I just love cats." Paige wondered if Mark found it as odd as she did that Chloe had stopped screaming at the exact moment Maria had opened the door. Regardless, she was relieved that she had finally settled down.

"What's her name?" Maria asked, poking her finger through the bar.

"Chloe," Paige replied, "but how did you know it was a she?"

"Oh, well, that's easy," Maria replied, facing Paige once again. "I read her mind." Confused, Paige glanced quickly at Mark, his expression mirroring her own.

"I'm sorry, did you say that you read my cat's mind?" Paige asked, disbelief clear in her tone. Laughing, Maria shook her head.

"I'm teasing. I guessed by the bright pink collar. I just assumed."

Slapping her forehead hard enough that she was sure she left a mark, Paige laughed, feeling the familiar rush of heat rising to her face. "Of course. I completely forgot."

When Maria suggested Mark get her bags while she showed Paige to her room, relief washed through her. For some reason she suddenly felt awkward and shy, very unlike her usual confident self. Nodding, Mark turned abruptly, while Paige followed Maria up one side of the enormous staircase. The walls were painted a beautiful taupe, and Paige recognized some of the artwork that had been hung strategically along the curves. She instantly fell in love with a piece called *The Newbury Marshes* as well as another by Henri Rousseau called *Tiger in a Tropical Storm*. Paige found it interesting that Mark would have several by this artist who was self-taught, once stating that 'all of nature' had been his teacher.

Once they reached the top of the stairs, Maria turned left. Speaking over her shoulder, she informed Paige that she would be in the Green Room. As Maria opened the door, Paige skidded to a stop just behind her. The room was spectacular. She felt as though she had just been catapulted into the most extraordinary secret garden. The walls were a pale moss, the lush carpet beneath her feet the same color. There were four large windows that looked out over the circular drive and well beyond. From here Paige could see the mountains in the distance, as well as a beautiful view of a stream that ran through the property. Until now, she had no idea it even existed. The four-poster bed was topped with a quilted muted floral coverlet, its greens and purples a perfect foil for its backdrop. The curtains were a pale lavender, extending from the high ceiling and ending in a luxurious pool on the floor. There was a plush settee together with a white vanity, a small, upholstered chair tucked beneath it. Walking over to the bed, Paige placed the carrier down on the floor, dropping her purse next to it. It was then that Paige observed Maria open a door that led to the private bathroom. If she thought her room was beautiful, the bathroom was breathtaking. At its very center was the largest clawfoot tub she had ever seen, and she thought she could soak in that beauty for hours. It was porcelain white, a perfect foil for the muted gray and white tile floor. The matching white dual sinks looked out across the same spectacular landscape. Here, however, the windows were covered in a luxurious white muslin fabric. In the far corner of the vast room was a white chaise longue, a sumptuous white robe lying to the side.

Open shelving revealed thick white towels, hand towels and facecloths. There were five oversized throw rugs that not only matched the bed coverlet, adding a refreshing pop of color, but whose thickness belied belief. The word decadent came to mind as Paige stared, unable to form a coherent thought. The toilet area had its own separate door, and the linen closet was filled to the brim with even more sumptuous towels as well as every sinfully scented boutique soap that Paige had ever seen outside of an actual store. Still mute, she followed Maria back out just as Mark arrived, face flushed with sweat, with two of her suitcases. Wiping his sleeve across his face he glanced quickly around the room.

"I hope this will be comfortable during your visit."

Paige's quick laugh came out more like a snort, an embarrassing quirk she wished would just go away. Since she was clearly destined to be embarrassed the entire time she would be here, she went with it.

"Oh Mark. This is nothing short of extraordinary," she exclaimed, spinning in a circle. "All of it is just so welcoming! May I ask who your designer was?"

"Designer?" he repeated, his expression perplexed. "I did this myself."

"You did this—" she marveled, spreading her arms wide to encompass the room, "yourself?" The disbelief in her voice sent a shaft of irritation through Mark. Clearly, she believed that people with money just automatically spent it on expensive designers. It was disappointing, he realized.

"Yes," he replied dryly. "All by myself." Turning, he spoke over his shoulder as he left the room. "I'm going to get the rest of your bags. Maria, please show her the area for her cat's litter box."

Confused by Mark's attitude, Paige shrugged it off. He was probably just tired and hot from carrying the suitcases. *They were heavy*, she thought, feeling guilty. Turning to Maria, she followed her pointed finger to a door by the vanity. Opening it, Paige could see it was a small closet. It was separate from the walk-in closet closest to the bathroom, which was the size of her bedroom at home. It was a much cozier space and perfect for all of Chloe's things. Clapping her hands, Paige smiled at Maria.

"Thank you for everything. It's all just too much." Laughing, Maria headed for the door just as Mark's head appeared at the top of the stairs. She watched him rest for a moment before bringing her last two bags to her room. Placing them next to the others, he took a deep breath, again wiping the sweat from his brow.

"I'm so sorry, Mark. I realize they are heavy," she stated, pointing to the pile of suitcases.

"Oh, not at all," he replied, his tone just shy of sarcastic. "I can understand how you would want to bring every single article of clothing you owned. One never knows what party one might get invited to." A flash of irritation at his tone, Paige drew herself up, eyes narrowed.

"For your information, I packed exactly zero party outfits. I'm here to work, in case you have forgotten. Also, I'm not from Montana," she spat, fire erupting from her violet eyes, "so I was unsure of what I would need. Had I known it would be too difficult for you to manage, I would have asked Maria to help me bring them up. She could have done all four at the same time no doubt!"

Maria, her head ricocheting from Paige to Mark, quietly slipped out of the room. Neither noticed.

Insulted, Mark stepped forward, glaring down at her. Her chest rose and fell with her agitation, but she didn't flinch as she met his eyes. Mark couldn't help getting lost in them. Angry, their color deepened, to the color of a ripe plum, he thought as his gaze slid to her lips. Suddenly the oxygen level in the room dipped dangerously low, and Paige sensed the shift in his gaze.

The kiss was sudden, passionate, and more than welcome.

This was what she had wanted from the first moment she had seen Mark standing on the front veranda. His lips slanted over hers, his tongue thrusting, meeting hers. It was a dance of pure, unbridled lust. Mark pulled her more firmly against him. Paige could feel his need as well as hers, which was coiled and hot. It was everything she wanted and everything she couldn't have. The thought hit her like a cold shower, and she broke from the kiss, pushing herself away. They both stood quietly, the sound of their labored breathing slowly becoming normal.

"I shouldn't have done that," Mark said, his expression regretful. "It was a mistake and I apologize."

"It was my mistake as well," Paige whispered, desperately trying to control the passion that raged through her. "I never become involved with clients. It's a rule and it will never happen again," she finished, determination in her voice.

"I see," Mark answered, curious to know who had hurt her, for it was clear to him that someone had. The thought that another man had visited this upon her caused Mark's gut to wrench. If he were honest, just the thought there was another man bothered him.

He felt ashamed that he had allowed his own unpleasant experience with a woman who only cared about his money to cloud his reasoning. She was not her. He needed to remember that.

"Agreed," Mark said. Reaching out, they shook hands firmly.

Smiling tenuously, Paige let out a relieved breath. *It's fine*, she thought. *It's under control. You're under control.*

Turning, Mark made his way out, informing her that Maria served dinner at six. "Just unpack and settle in," he offered, his hand on the doorknob. "Come down whenever you're ready. I want you to treat this home like your own."

"Thank you, Mark. I will be down as soon as I'm unpacked and freshened up." With a curt nod, Mark quietly closed the door, leaving Paige alone with her thoughts. Immediately she let Chloe out and after setting up her litter box and food dishes, which had taken up one entire suitcase, she threw herself back onto the king-sized bed. Sinking the luxurious softness, Paige spread her arms wide. Her gaze found the ceiling, as she tried to digest what had just happened. The attraction to Mark was undeniable, and now she knew he felt it as well.

She knew she was in dangerous territory, remembering that this was how it had all started with Kyle. But a tiny voice in her head kept reminding her that Mark was not Kyle. Clearly Mark was a man of character and kindness. Kyle had been angry with her when she had rescued Chloe, saying that animals carried disease and smelled. They had a terrible fight, but ultimately, she had kept Chloe, although Kyle insisted he wouldn't sleep at her apartment.

Shaking her head, Paige thrust the memory aside. She was here in this beautiful home and Mark was going to make their gallery an enormous amount of money, although this time the money didn't excite her as it had in the past. This time was different, but she couldn't quite put her finger on why. Suddenly she felt the bed move as Chloe jumped up, walking daintily to where Paige lay. Stroking her soft fur, Paige closed her eyes, allowing herself a moment to relax. Before she knew it, she was sound asleep, Chloe curled up beside her, purring loudly. When she awoke a short time later, she refused to acknowledge that she had dreamt about Mark. After all, it was only a dream.

CHAPTER 5

PAIGE CHANGED INTO A PAIR OF LOOSE LINEN PANTS WITH A LIGHT sweater before heading downstairs. She could hear voices and observed Mark and another gentleman talking in the living room. The man had his back to her, and as she descended, he turned. Smiling, Paige made her way towards them, sniffing the air as she did so. Something smelled delicious, and her stomach growled in response. It occurred to her that she hadn't eaten since early this morning and now it was close to five-thirty.

Mark smiled, and something warm and cozy pulsed through her. She barely looked at the other man until Mark began the introductions. Reluctantly, she turned away from Mark, giving the stranger her full attention. Standing almost as tall as Mark, he nodded as he offered his hand. Paige couldn't help but notice how extremely handsome he was, although he appeared younger than herself. Instantly, she felt a sisterly inclination.

"Adrian, this is Paige Liston, the curator I told you about. Paige, this is Adrian Lawrence. He manages the day-to-day care and handling of the horses."

"So nice to meet you, Adrian," she responded, making her way to one of the large chairs. Both men waited until she was seated, then sat on opposite ends of the couch. Adrian had been around horses all his life and lived with his parents at a neighboring ranch. As she suspected, he was just nineteen, and this was his first actual job. Soon they were all sharing stories about their backgrounds as they listened to the sounds coming from the kitchen. Maria was busy along with a young woman whom Paige assumed was one of the staff hired by Maria. Paige had offered to help, but she had been quickly shooed away.

"You are the guest," she replied warmly. "This is my job and I'm happy to do it."

Overhearing their conversation, Mark was impressed. Paige hadn't needed to offer to help, but clearly, she had felt the desire to do so. Again, he couldn't help comparing her actions to those of his previous girlfriend. She had proven to be a gold digger, and it had nearly broken him. Shaking his head, he quickly rid himself of the thought. Soon, dinner was ready, and they all made their way to the large dining table. It was perfectly set, and Paige was starving. Maria had made a traditional Cuban dish of Arroz Con Pollo which consisted of chicken, rice, onions, herbs and spices. Paige unapologetically had two plates full before finally being satisfied. After dinner she sat back, too full to move. Paige was utterly exhausted but followed as Mark and Adrian made their way out to the veranda to enjoy some coffee. Choosing a rocker, Paige sat, staring up at the night sky. She didn't remember the stars being so big or appearing so close when she took the time to observe them in New York, which she thought, sadly, was not very often. The air was cool, and Paige shivered slightly. Seeing her discomfort, Adrian offered her his jacket. Grateful, she wrapped it firmly around her shoulders. Glancing at Mark, he appeared annoyed. Wondering what had upset him, Paige observed the look he directed at Adrian as he sat back down. It almost seemed as though he was angry that Adrian had given her his jacket.

That couldn't be it, she admonished herself. *How ridiculous. Why would he care?* Adrian was just a boy for crying out loud. Convinced she had misinterpreted the entire exchange, Paige settled back once more, burrowing into the warm jacket. Maria had joined them, however her junior assistant had gone on to bed as she was a student at the community college and needed to study.

No one spoke, each satisfied with their own thoughts as they observed the night sky. Paige tried to relax but was too aware of Mark, who sat just a few chairs from her. She could feel his stare, and more than once their eyes had met. The chemistry between them was intense, and Paige once again replayed their kiss in her mind. She would be lying if she said she didn't want it to happen again. The truth was, she wanted his kiss, and so much more. Reminding herself once again why that couldn't happen, Paige became restless. Suddenly she needed to put space between herself and his distinct maleness. Standing suddenly, she walked over to Adrian, handing him his jacket.

"I apologize, everyone, but I'm just so very exhausted and well," she continued, searching for a viable excuse for her abrupt departure, "Chloe is alone so I'm going to head to bed." She was talking too quickly and sounded semi hysterical even to her own ear. Both men rose instantly. Nodding, they all said goodnight, their expressions a mix of concern and puzzlement. Paige climbed the stairs quickly, eager to be alone.

Later, snuggled under the covers, Chloe by her feet purring softly, Paige reinforced her decision to maintain a strictly professional relationship. She could not continue to allow just his proximity to affect her like that, she brooded. He was just a man, she told herself firmly. After all, weren't there just a plethora of good-looking men in New York who were not her client? Of course there were, and with that final thought swirling, she fell fast asleep and dreamt of Mark. Again.

. . .

THE NEXT MORNING, PAIGE AWOKE TO A SOFT KNOCK. "COME IN," she directed as she sat, pulling the quilt up around her.

"Good morning," Maria hummed, her smile brilliant. Carrying a tray, she made her way to the vanity, placing it down. "It's a beautiful morning out there today," she announced as she opened the French doors leading to the veranda. Slipping out of bed, Paige grabbed her robe, belting it as she made her way outside. Standing at the railing, she watched as Maria placed the tray onto a small round table flanked by two chairs. Paige closed her eyes, the powerful aroma of coffee beckoning her.

"Maria, you really didn't need to do this. I'm perfectly capable of coming down and getting my coffee and breakfast." Taking the pot and cup off the tray, as well as a small pitcher of cream, Maria placed everything carefully on the table.

"It's your first morning here, and I wanted you to get the full effect," she returned, waving her arms expansively over the vista. "Besides, as I have said before, it is my job and my pleasure." With that, she let herself out, leaving Paige to wonder at the beauty that surrounded her. July in Montana was breathtaking, the mountains in the distance proud and ever watchful. Paige found it odd that she never really noticed them the first time she was here, she thought, sipping her coffee appreciatively. Suddenly, a flash of silver caught in her peripheral vision and garnered her attention. Mark. She knew it was him immediately, despite the distance.

It was then that she noticed the vertical jumps set at different intervals. Mark had explained to her previously that he liked having them so that the horses were exercised properly. Mesmerized, she observed as horse and rider jumped seamlessly, over and over. After each landing, Mark would bend over Storm Cloud, rubbing his hand along his neck. The love between man and beast was captivating to witness.

She realized she had been holding her coffee cup to her lips, so intent in her perusal that she forgot to sip it. *Great, you're so besotted you can't manage to finish your coffee,* she thought, finally taking a gulp. *You really need to do better,* she told herself, even as she continued to follow Mark's every move like a hawk with its prey in sight.

Feeling something warm against her leg, Paige looked down. Chloe was up, weaving between her legs. "Well my girl, it's time to get dressed and check out my client's work," she announced, reaching down to offer a quick chin scratch. Finishing her coffee and bagel, she rose. *Today,* she reminded herself firmly, *you are meeting with your client.* "Client," she repeated out loud. Feeling a newfound resolve, Paige dressed, ready to fall into her role as a curator. Now, if only her body and runaway heart wouldn't get in the way.

PAIGE HAD BEEN GIVEN A TOUR THE PREVIOUS DAY, SO SHE HEADED directly to the mudroom off the kitchen. The door took her out to the back veranda. From there, several paths led to the stables. The sun was warm but comfortable. She had chosen a pair of denim shorts and a sleeveless top. Deciding sneakers would be the best way to go, she had grabbed her favorite pair. As she strolled casually along the dirt path, it was suddenly clear that the area of land that Mark owned was enormous. She hadn't asked but was curious as to how much there actually was. As she approached the large stable doors, Mark stepped out, a harness in his hand. Seeing her, he waved, smiling, as he headed towards her. Her heart began to hammer against her chest immediately. Once again, her body betrayed her. Just seeing him caused a low coil of tension to work its way through her. He wore denim pants with a short-sleeved black polo. A brown belt and cowboy boots completed the look. Paige had been to plenty of fashion shows featuring the highest paid male models in the business, and they had virtually nothing over Mark. His masculinity was raw, oozing from his every pore. His walk was confident and commanding. There wasn't a single aspect of him that was even remotely contrived. She could see that his hair was wet with sweat, his arms layered with a fine film of dust. Coming to a stop in front of her, she looked up, her breath catching in her throat. *Good grief*, she thought, *he's magnificent.*

"Good morning, Paige," he greeted her, rubbing off some of the dirt from his forearms as he came to a stop in front of her. "I was on my way back to the house to shower but since you're here, would you like a tour of the stables?"

Nodding her head enthusiastically, Paige fell into step with Mark as he turned, making his way back inside.

"Did you sleep well last night?" he asked, his expression concerned. "You seemed pretty beat."

"I did. Thank you. I'm afraid the hours of flying and, well, just the excitement finally caught up with me." Also, the excitement of seeing him again, she thought.

"Good, I'm glad. I just finished working with Storm Cloud. Would you like to meet him?"

A thrill ran along Paige's spine. Finally, she would meet the subject of Mark's brilliant painting. In a way, he had brought them both together.

The wooden stable was enormous, with fifteen barn stalls on each side. As they made their way inside, the smells of fresh hay and sweet grass assailed her senses. There was a large tack room that they passed, as well as an area to hose the horses down. Above them, the loft ran the entire length of the stable with ladders placed strategically to climb up. They continued down, the soft whinny of the other horses following them as they passed. Finally, she stood before Storm Cloud's stall, and nothing could have prepared her for the sheer majesty that was this stallion.

He was enormous, standing at seventeen hands, which, as Mark explained, was large for a thoroughbred. His coat was a molten silver, shiny and smooth. Upon seeing Mark, Storm

Cloud nickered softly, pushing his nose through the bars. Mark reached his hand through, stroking his nose. Paige could only stare in awe at this proud and majestic creature. Suddenly he looked directly at her, and Paige felt a shock run through her. His eyes were crystalline blue, and the effect was arresting. He was extraordinarily intelligent, and Paige knew immediately he was assessing her. It was a test that one could not study for, so she simply waited, unable to look away. Then, as if his decision was made, he tossed his magnificent head up and down several times, stomping his hooves loudly. Uncertain, she glanced over at Mark.

"I believe you have met with his approval," he said, reaching out once more to rub Storm Cloud's nose. When he smiled at his horse, Paige felt a sudden weakness in her knees, followed by an unexpected flash of jealousy. It was a complete surprise and Paige shook her head to dispel the emotion. Still, she knew that had that smile been directed at her, every ounce of self-control in every single cell of her body would not have been nearly enough to prevent her from catapulting headlong into his arms.

"Really?" she breathed, unable to speak any more words.

"Absolutely. I would also like to point out that he doesn't like anyone, even Adrian." With a slight laugh, he turned, directing them out of the stable. Paige couldn't help but look backwards once more, only to observe Storm Cloud wink. Stumbling slightly, she blinked furiously several times, sure it had been a play of the light. Glancing back towards Mark she decided to keep it to herself, afraid she would sound like a lunatic. Although she was pretty sure that ship had already sailed.

"He gets to you, doesn't he," Mark observed, a statement rather than a question.

"Actually, yes, he does," Paige replied, understanding immediately what Mark was referring to.

"It's a kind of kindred connection," Mark continued as they stepped into the sunshine. Turning to face her he said, "If I'm being truthful, Paige, I feel the same thing with you." Stunned, she was helpless to stop what she knew was going to happen. He gently placed his finger under her chin, lifting it until she had no choice but to look directly at him. "I haven't stopped thinking about you or that kiss. I'm no schoolboy," he continued, "but with you I feel my self-control slip."

"Mark, please," Paige pleaded, her body already preparing itself for him, as though her permission was unnecessary. "I can't do this, not again. I won't ever go through that again."

"Whoever he is," Mark replied, gently, "I'm not him." His expression sympathetic, he moved closer. "Give me an opportunity to show you who I really am."

"I'm afraid. How will I ever really know that you are who you say you are?"

"Stop talking, Paige," he whispered, his voice husky with passion, "and kiss me." She watched, mesmerized, as his head bent, her eyes closing just as his lips met hers. The sparks were once again instantaneous, electric. His hands moved from her slim shoulders to her waist. Paige stepped fully into the embrace, her trembling hands snaking around his neck, seeking him hungrily. Her breasts were taut and solid against his hard chest. She knew it was a mistake, yet, once again, found herself helpless to resist him.

"Ahem, um, I'm sorry to interrupt, boss—"

They broke apart violently, their breathing rapid from their interrupted passion.

Running his hand through his hair, Mark whirled around, his expression one of sheer frustration.

"What is it?" Mark barked, still trying to restrain his lust.

Backing up a step, Adrian appeared uncertain, his cowboy hat twirling between his nervous hands.

Observing the fear in the boy's eyes, Mark lowered his voice. "I'm sorry, Adrian," he apologized. "Is there a problem?" he continued; his manner decidedly friendlier.

Relaxing his shoulders, Adrian nodded in Paige's direction before answering.

"It's Lilly," he began pointing towards the stable. "I'm pretty sure she has a nail and was wondering if you wanted me to get the doc out here."

Mark was instantly at attention, worry crossing his features.

"Yes, call him right now. I will go have a look at it myself as well." As they watched him leave, Mark turned to Paige, his tone apologetic. "I'm sorry but I'm afraid this is an urgent matter."

"No, of course, go," Page responded, disappointed and relieved. "I understand perfectly."

"I'd like to pick up where we left off later. Maybe dinner? In town? Just the two of us?"

Hesitating, Paige finally answered.

"Mark, this is not a good idea." As he began to speak, she quickly interrupted him. "No, I mean it. It isn't. I'm not the girl that takes risks and this would be taking too much of a chance. This has happened before" she began, hesitantly. "With another client. It was a mistake; he was a mistake. I'm sorry but please, I'm asking you to respect my decision."

"I see," Mark responded, his disappointment evident. "I see that you are incapable of taking me at face value. Your inability to refrain from comparing me to your ex is more than obvious. I suppose I should have conducted myself differently. Maybe that would have helped you to distinguish the difference between he and I."

Without another word he spun, his frustration obvious in the rigid set to his shoulders. Paige stood for a few moments, watching him go, fighting tears.

She wondered why he couldn't understand, exasperation and hurt at war within her. She wasn't comparing him to Kyle, was she? As she made her way back to the house, it occurred to her that maybe Mark was right. Maybe it wasn't because Mark was her client.

Maybe it went deeper than that. At that moment, Paige wondered if she could ever trust any other man. It had been two years, and she had made an excuse every time a man tried to get close. It hadn't really mattered before, but now there was this man, and suddenly, Paige realized with a sinking sensation, it mattered very, very much.

CHAPTER 6

Mark made his way back into the stable, cursing under his breath. "Leave it to me to pick yet another emotionally unavailable female," he grumbled. It was becoming the story of his life. Finding out that his ex-girlfriend was a gold digger had been devastating, however, since then he had been unable to connect on any level with any other woman. It appears they either knew about his wealth and chased him unabashedly, or, upon seeing his home, immediately began planning their wedding.

More than that, though, he had found no one that truly understood his love for all animals and his determination to save as many as he could. Until Paige. It was clear that she loved animals as well and certainly she had a heart for them as she had rescued Chloe. But more than that, he had witnessed for himself her unique ability to connect on a much deeper level. Her response to Storm Cloud and his to her had assured him it was sincere.

Paige also did not appear to be overly impressed by his wealth, even though she had shared that she had grown up poor. Still, she seemed overly enthusiastic about anything brand name. He recognized her purses, as well as some clothing she wore were from expensive designer labels. It left open a sliver of doubt that she was, in fact, the real thing. Not that it was necessarily a terrible thing or a character flaw, only, he wondered if she could be equally content without it. His father had always told Mark to remain humble, feet planted firmly on the ground, but his dreams needed to fly. Wealth, his father had advised, could come and it could go. Neither would matter, however, if you carried your happiness within. Then, your circumstances could never define you. He needed to know that Paige could be happy in wealth, and in poverty. Even if he were completely sure of her motivation, her reluctance to have any kind of romantic relationship ended the possibility of knowing for sure.

Mark was ready for forever, wanting to fill his home with children and dogs, with Chloe's approval first of course, and all manner of beasts, but he wasn't willing to settle. In fact, he refused to settle. If Paige wanted a professional relationship, he was fully prepared to comply with her wishes.

The next several weeks passed without incident. Paige and Mark were civil, neither referring to their shared kisses. Paige had never felt more miserable. Mark had created a space in one of the spare rooms of his stable to paint in. Everything he needed from canvas to paints to the very best brushes were at his disposal. Paige had wondered why, when he had a substantial number of unused rooms in his home, he chose to paint there. When she had questioned him, he had simply shrugged. "I feel inspired there. I can see the mountains, my horses, and breathe in the fresh air. It's where I feel most at home." Still, the house was simply enormous and to Paige's way of thinking, beautiful enough to inspire anyone.

One afternoon, fighting boredom, she had decided to explore the home further, walking from room to room. There had been no fewer than ten bedrooms, six bathrooms and a media room that she hadn't even known existed. Much of the time, she found herself taking cooking lessons from Maria and had finally met her assistant, Emily. She was very sweet, and Paige had instantly taken her under her wing. Just eighteen, she was working her way through college. Her parents lived in town and, like Adrian, this was her first genuine job. She did much of the cleaning and assisted with dinner each evening. Both she and Maria had their own rooms on the first floor.

Mark was now working on his third piece, and Paige marveled at his pace. Most of her clients would take as long as three months just to do one piece. It worried her somewhat, He hadn't wanted her to see the new paintings, which had turned out to be a point of contention between them. As the curator, she was responsible for examining all the artwork being created. Unfortunately, there had been those who had tried to defraud them by handing in work from unknown artists as their own. She didn't believe this to be the case with Mark, however, she was becoming annoyed by his aloof attitude. Feeling particularly irritated, she decided to make her way to the stable and confront him once again. This time she was determined not to leave until he showed her at least one of the three completed pieces. Emboldened by her newfound determination, Paige strode purposely to the stable, walking directly to the closed door where she knocked, loudly, three times. She heard his hushed curse and stumbled back when he flung the door open, allowing it to crash into the wall. Startled, she simply stared at him for a moment, her eyes blinking furiously. His hair was running in every direction imaginable. He wore a blue denim shirt that was covered in various shades of paint, some of it finding its way to his cheek. His angry glare prompted an equally angry response. Pointing her finger, she fumed.

"I need to see one of those paintings, and I will not leave until I have. You will not continue to ignore me. You're getting paid a pretty penny, Mr. Richards," she spit out, "and my job is to make sure our investment remains secure."

Breathing heavily, Paige fixed her angry glare directly into his heaven-sent eyes, her arms crossed defiantly.

"Is that right?" Mark drawled; his expression having gone from angry to amused as he leaned casually against the door frame. "And just exactly what are you planning to do if I say no?"

Looking past him, she could see the canvas he was currently working on; however, it was covered with a bright blue tarp. She assumed the large, covered squares stacked backwards against the wall, each wrapped in a cloth canvas, were his completed works. Her exasperation mounting, she stomped her foot, hands clenched tightly by her sides. She hadn't foot-stomped since she had been a child and the fact that this egotistical, self-righteous, incredibly sexy beast of man had driven her to this point brought her to the very brink of insanity.

Without thinking, she stepped inches from him. Surprised, he looked into her determined eyes and before Mark knew what was happening, she reached up, placing her hands firmly behind his head, then, standing on tiptoes she pulled him in for the sexiest kiss he had ever experienced. His initial shock soon gave way to passion as he pulled her tightly against him. Walking them both backwards, he kicked the door shut, leaving them in complete privacy. It was as though the floodgates had opened as Paige melted into him. Mark's hands moved slowly downwards, stopping as he cupped her buttocks, kneading them lovingly. Her excitement was beyond anything she had ever felt before, and she never wanted it to end. Suddenly, he lifted her and she instinctively wrapped her legs around his waist. Their lips remained locked in a lustful dance until he pulled away, his breathing harsh in her ear. She placed her head into his neck, then, releasing her hands, slowly slid down his body. Paige had never felt such abject disappointment in herself.

"That was unacceptable," she whispered, desperate for the passion still coursing through her body to subside. "I realize I'm sending mixed messages and I'm embarrassed by my behavior, Mark. You deserve better than that."

His expression perplexed, Mark lifted her chin, looking deep into her eyes.

"That kiss was mutual, as much my doing as yours," he said kindly. "You don't have to be so hard on yourself, Paige. What's happening between us is completely natural. Our attraction is powerful, and we acted on it."

Stepping back, Paige wrapped her arms around herself.

"Mark, I made a mistake once with another client. A terrible mistake that is still haunting me. I could have lost everything had my employer been anyone other than the man of character that he is. My reputation took a hit, and I just can't chance that again. I have worked so hard to get where I am. It isn't you personally and I'm terribly sorry that I gave that impression to you earlier."

"Someone betrayed me as well," Mark confided, his voice laced with sympathy. "I thought we were in love, deeply in love, but it turned out that it was my bank account she wanted, not me."

"I'm so sorry, Mark," Paige breathed, her expression sorrowful. "I can't imagine how much that must have hurt."

Shrugging dismissively, Mark made his way to the completed canvases.

"I was over her a long time ago," he answered. "Since then, I have simply kept my guard up. The truth is, we may never be sure of each other's true intentions. You don't know that I won't be like him, and I don't know if you will be like her, but, as my parents always told me, that is where faith comes in." Before she could respond, Mark pulled the cloth cover off the painting he held.

"You are right about one thing, however," he said before handing her the canvas. "This is a job, and we will move forward as only business partners if that is truly how you feel. I would never force you or try to sway you." Eyeing the painting she held, he continued.

"Go ahead and look at them all. If you don't like them, let me know. Hopefully, they will meet your high standards." With that, he opened the door. Not waiting for her response, he closed it quietly behind him.

Paige stood for some time, not moving, thinking about everything he had said. She wanted to cry and to scream and to run after him, all at the same time. *But he's right,* she thought. *This is my job; he is a client and you have work to do.*

Slowly, she turned the first canvas so it faced her. It was ethereal, too perfect for this world. In it, a stream ran through a wooded copse. Across the gently running water stood a horse, his head just about to slip in to quench its thirst but its attention was focused across the stream. The eyes captured her. Their glow otherworldly, intense, their focus on some unknown entity. *They pierce the soul* Paige thought. Not Storm Cloud, this horse was the color of honey, its hooves and powerful chest, white. It had a saddle on, the reins pulled off to the side, held by the rider who was not depicted. Paige felt as though it were she standing on the other side, that it was she who had captured this magnificent beast's attention. Shivers ran along her arms as she absorbed every stroke of paint, every curve of the horse. Every plant and flower lovingly created and brought to life. This is what she lived for. The kind of art that made you feel something, made you laugh or cry or scream or just made you feel alive. That is what this painting did. She had been right about Mark. He was a genius, an artistic phenomenon. And she had discovered him.

Pressing the canvas against her chest, she closed her eyes tightly. Now, more than ever, she had to distance herself from Mark. He was going to do great things, and she couldn't be the reason he faltered. Guilt ran through her as she remembered how she had thrown herself at Mark. Suddenly she didn't want to see the other paintings. Clearly Mark was a brilliant artist, certainly the greatest she had ever known. She would remain here on the ranch, however, until he finished the last piece. Only then would she look at the rest. She also decided to keep that to herself. As for her feelings for Mark, she needed to bury them. It was clear to her that she was falling in very deep like with him and there could be no happy ending for them. Kyle had taught her that there really wasn't any such thing.

CHAPTER 7

JUMPING OFF THE BED, PAIGE CLAPPED HER HANDS EXCITEDLY. Bending, she picked Chloe up, whirling her gently while she kissed her soft head. Camilla was coming to visit, and she couldn't be happier.

It had been desperately dismal for the last week. She and Mark barely spoke, only in each other's company at dinner. Maria had tried everything to put them together, but with little success. Mark was polite but distant, as was she, although, more than once, she had found herself daydreaming about him, remembering how his lips and hands had felt on her body. It had come to her attention that his suite of rooms was also on the second floor, at the end of the enormous upstairs hallway. Realizing how close he was had been pure torture. Lying in bed at night she had fantasized about sneaking into his room, sliding into his bed, naked. Sometimes the fantasies had been so intense she had to jump into a cold shower for a few minutes.

Shaking off her present gloom and doom mentality, Paige made her way downstairs to be sure Mark was amenable to Camilla's visit. She didn't want to make any assumptions. This was, after all, Mark's home. She was simply a temporary guest. As

Paige rounded the last step, she quickly skidded to a stop when she realized Mark had company. The woman sat facing Mark, her long legs crossed at the ankles. She was young, incredibly stunning, her hair a glorious mass of red that fell to her tiny waist. She wore a Kelly-green sweater over a black A-line skirt. Paige recognized her gorgeous black Jimmy Choo shoes. Hearing her approach, Paige faltered as the woman locked eyes with hers, venom in their emerald green depths. Standing, Mark turned towards Paige as she timidly entered the room.

"Mark, I apologize," she began, glancing with uncertainty once more at the beautiful stranger. "I didn't realize you had company."

As she approached, she noted how miserable he appeared. Whoever his guest was, he wasn't thrilled that she was there.

"No, no. It's fine. Please, have a seat," he directed, pointing to the couch.

Paige could feel the woman's angry glare directed at her as she sat. Scooting to the edge of the cushion, she folded her hands nervously, placing them on her lap.

Clearing his throat, Mark made the introductions.

"Paige, this is Liza," he began, waving his hand in her direction. "She's an old friend," he coughed out nervously. "Liza, this is Paige. She's a curator from New York, representing Roja Galleries. I'm doing some paintings for them," he finished, grabbing a glass of water from the coffee table, gulping most of it down.

"Roja Galleries?" Liza questioned; eyebrows raised. "Goodness, that's such a prestigious gallery."

Nodding, Paige agreed.

"Yes, it is and of course I'm so thrilled to be working with Mark. He has such extraordinary talent."

"Does he really?" she drawled, fixing her attention once more on Mark. "You used to tell me it was just scribbling," she continued, irritation seeping into her voice.

Glancing at Mark, Paige waited for his reply, but he remained silent.

"Also," Liza continued, ignoring the awkward silence, "Mark and I were more than friends, weren't we, Mark?" she finished, a sly smile revealing the whitest teeth Paige had ever seen. "In fact, we were actually engaged to be married once."

Suddenly, it all made sense. This was Mark's ex-fiancée, the one that had broken his heart. No wonder he looks so defeated. She felt a sudden rush of sympathy for Mark. Clearly, he had had no idea that she would just show up.

Paige now understood Liza's animosity towards her. After all, Paige admitted, I'm not bad looking. Surely it must have been jarring for her to have seen me coming down the stairs from where Mark's bedroom was located. It occurred to her that Liza really did not know what the nature of their relationship was, which gave Paige an idea. If she was wrong, Mark would kick her out on her rear, but if she was right, he might just give her one extra canvas as a thank you.

Taking a deep breath for courage, Paige faced Liza, her gaze direct.

"Mark is just too humble for his own good," Paige purred. Without looking away, she found Mark's arm, gently running her hand along its length. Liza's eyes narrowed, sparks of jealousy traveling at an alarming trajectory focused directly on Paige. Afraid to see Mark's reaction, she continued, her words dripping honey. "Thankfully, he allowed me to convince him of how absolutely brilliant he is," sending her best version of a loving glance in his direction. Paige heard Mark's chuckle, which he quickly covered with a cough. Relieved that he wasn't angry, Paige once again directed her attention towards Liza, whose skin tone had taken on a decidedly sickly pallor. "I'm afraid I can't let you see any of the work as it's gallery property and right now Mark and I just want to enjoy the creative process, however, we would love it if you could perhaps come to dinner sometime?" Without waiting for her response, Paige continued, leaning her head into Mark's shoulder. "Maria makes the most delicious chicken I have ever had." A frozen smile fixed on her face that fell well short of her eyes, Liza stood abruptly.

"I'm afraid I can't stay," she hissed. "I have plans with my—er —with someone later. I just happened to be in the neighborhood." Gathering her purse, she shot Paige a furious glare.

"Mark, it was wonderful to see you again," she mumbled, practically breaking into a jog as she made for the door. Stepping onto the veranda, she made her way to her car, never once turning back in their direction. Mark and Paige stood watching her until long after she disappeared from view.

Paige was scared to death to look at him. She had just effectively rid him of the woman he had once loved, and she wasn't sure he had been ready for that. Paige was well into second guessing her actions when she suddenly observed Mark's shoulders shaking. Glancing quickly, she could see that he was laughing, quietly at first, then quickly escalating to a roar. His infectious laugh was contagious and soon Paige found herself doubled over as well. Both were holding their stomachs, tears running down their faces. Finally, Mark took her hand, leading them both to two large rockers. Seated, they sat in companionable silence for a few minutes, enjoying the cool breeze. It was close to September, and Paige no longer wore any summer clothes.

"Why did you do that, Paige?" Mark asked quietly.

A full minute passed before Paige answered, and when she did, she kept her gaze fastened on the distant mountaintops. They had a remarkable calming effect and right now, her heart racing, she desperately needed that.

"If I'm honest, I did it because she hurt you. She hurt you and that made me angry."

"I see." When a few minutes passed without him saying anything further, Paige turned. He, too, had his eyes fixed on the horizon, and she wondered briefly if they made him feel the same way.

Fidgeting, Paige finally broke the silence.

"I'm sorry Mark, if you felt it was presumptuous. It was none of my business. I hope you can for—"

"Thank you," he interrupted, facing her. "She showed up unannounced and I hadn't seen her since the breakup. I heard that the much wealthier version she left me for apparently found a younger version of her. So, in the end, I guess she learned the hard way. Although," he continued, turning his attention once more towards the quickly sinking sun, "maybe not, since it was clear she was trying her luck with me again. I was completely lost as to how to proceed until you took over. I'm not a man that usually gets lost," he finished, exhaling deeply.

"Well, in that case, you're welcome," Paige answered, pleased that he was grateful. "It was absolutely my pleasure," she finished, laughter in her voice. Just then, the front door opened, and Maria stepped out.

"I have something special planned for lunch later so I hope you two stick around," she advised, as she walked over, pulling her sweater more tightly around her shoulders.

"I have been wondering all day what those wonderful aromas are," Paige responded enthusiastically.

"I have prepared for you my Cuban pernil which is a lovely slow roasted pork. It is my grandmother's recipe and sure to please."

Clapping her hands, Paige's eyes lit up. You wouldn't know by observing her slim build, but she loved to eat. The fact that Maria was Cuban meant that she brought the flavors of her heritage to the table. "Lucky for me," Paige thought happily.

Mark smiled at her enthusiasm. Standing, they both followed Maria back into the house, watching as she made her way back into the kitchen. Suddenly Paige's eyes widened, a look of dismay crossing her features.

"I completely forgot that I had something to ask you earlier!" Paige announced.

Chuckling, Mark replied.

"Yes, well, there was quite a lot happening at the time," he reminded her.

Nodding, Paige smiled nervously.

"Well, I was wondering, if it isn't too much to ask, that is, if my friend Camilla could come for a visit? She's a wonderful person and you won't even know that she is here," Paige promised, her expressive eyes beseeching.

"Paige," Mark replied impatiently, "I have told you several times. My home is your home while you are here. As such, you may invite anyone you please to come and stay."

"Well, I most certainly will not do so without consulting you first," she stated emphatically. "What if I just had friends come and one day you see random strangers roaming through your home. Surely that would cause some confusion."

Contemplating her words for a moment, Mark nodded.

"I see your point," he conceded, smiling. "How about you just inform me when someone is coming, so, as you say, I'm not caught off guard by random wandering strangers."

"Perfect," Paige gushed, excited at the prospect of having her friend coming for a visit. "I'm going to call her right now," she sang over her shoulder as she made her way upstairs to her room.

MARK STOOD FOR A FEW MOMENTS WATCHING HER TAKE THE STAIRS two at a time, his heart lodged somewhere in his throat. Every part of him wanted her. Today, the fact that she had helped him out of an awkward situation had blown him away. She had jumped in just to help him with virtually no way of knowing how it would turn out, reacting out of pure instinct. She was both beautiful and courageous.

The truth was, until he had seen Liza face to face, he hadn't been entirely sure that he was over her. But he had felt nothing but pity when he realized how desperate she must have been to seek him out again. She had to have known that even if he had feelings left, he would never take her back, knowing who she really was. Everything about her was artifice. But Paige, he ruminated, Paige had depth. As he turned to head out to the stables to check on Adrian before dinner, it occurred to him he really was ready for love again. He was ready for forever, but unfortunately, the woman he believed was meant for him still didn't know it. Somehow Mark had to convince her, the sooner the better, as he could barely keep his hands off her. Client or not, they were meant to be together.

AFTER PAIGE CALLED CAMILLA, SHE LAY BACK ON THE BED, CHLOE by her side, purring softly. She went over the events of the day, replaying every word, and wondered at her own audacity. She still couldn't believe that she had taken such an enormous risk. Yet an emotion she had yet to identify had driven her to act so outrageously. Once she had realized who Liza was and had observed her pompous, self-centered display, she couldn't help herself. However, if she were honest, she could have ignored all of that but for how it was affecting Mark. She didn't stop to ask herself why the thought of Mark being hurt had elicited such a powerful reaction. Liza had come to get her claws back into him, and he was too much of a gentleman to know how to handle it. Clearly, he had been out of his depth and knowing him as she did, he would never use his words to purposely hurt anyone. It was a trait in him she genuinely admired. He was kind. Truly kind.

Suddenly, a flash of memory shot through her mind. Kyle, mocking the outfit that she had chosen for her very first gallery presentation. It was a huge night for her, one that could determine her place in the New York art world's high society. Paul had placed all his faith in her, and she had so desperately wanted to be a success. When she had walked out of her bedroom wearing the simple black Ralph Lauren dress, Kyle had looked at her slowly, beginning with her hair and gradually making his way down. It was one of his favorite ways to humiliate her. His face had taken on a pinched expression, as though he had suddenly caught the scent of something putrid. It had devastated Paige, rooted her in shame. Ultimately, she had changed, but later, at the event, one of New York's greatest artistic benefactors had pulled her aside. She had been exceedingly kind when she had pointed out that such events required more of a simple, elegant garment, not the overly glittery, low-cut concoction that Kyle had insisted would be exactly right. "Next time try something simple and black, my dear," she had advised as she turned, gliding back towards the party. "Ralph Lauren would be perfect for you."

Pulling herself from the memory, Paige shook her head to dispel the negative emotions rolling through her. *It's over*, she thought. *He can't hurt you anymore.* Sighing heavily, she wondered if she would ever truly be ready for love again.

CHAPTER 8

THREE DAYS LATER PAIGE STOOD ON THE VERANDA WAVING WILDLY as she watched Camilla pull into the circular driveway. Unable to wait, she raced down the steps and grabbed her friend before she had fully exited the vehicle. Laughing, Camilla finally managed to get herself completely extricated and hugged her friend back. The two stood apart, each scanning the other to be sure all was well, then, with another quick hug, they headed inside.

"Oh, wait!" Camilla exclaimed, turning back towards her rental. "I completely forgot my bags!" Pulling her back towards the door, Paige assured her that Mark would be more than happy to help.

"Ah, so I finally get to meet your newest protégé," she teased as they walked through the door. Camilla stopped abruptly, her gaping mouth and wide eyes eliciting a burst of giggles from Paige.

"Pretty extraordinary, right?" Paige queried as she watched her friend try to absorb the opulent surroundings.

"You weren't kidding when you said this place was a mansion," Camilla exclaimed, still trying to absorb the enormity of the home. Just then, a deep voice interrupted.

"I see she finally made it," Mark announced as he made his way down the stairs. "Your friend has been beside herself waiting for you," he finished. As he approached the two women, he held out his hand, a welcoming smile revealing his gorgeous white teeth, a perfect foil to his tanned, chiseled features. Smiling widely, Camilla swung her hair back flirtatiously before extending her hand in greeting.

"So, you are the great and talented Mark Richards," she teased, unable to take her eyes off Mark. "I have heard wonderful things about you," she continued, still shaking Mark's hand. Seeing her instant adoration, Paige suddenly felt a flash of jealousy. She didn't like the way her friend was looking at Mark, and she certainly didn't like the way he was looking at Camilla. Suddenly she found herself feeling agitated.

"Yes, well, Camilla, this is Mark, and Mark, Camilla," she interrupted abruptly, pulling her friend's hand from Mark's, propelling her towards the stairs. "Let me show you your room. It's stunning," Paige babbled, a hint of hysteria clear in her voice. Perplexed, Camilla considered her friend, a sudden look of understanding crossing her features. A small smile playing around her lips, she inquired about her bags as she turned to face Mark.

"I'll take care of it," he said, confused by Paige's quick departure. She was practically carrying her friend up the stairs. Shaking his head, he made his way outside, hopeful that Camilla travelled considerably lighter than her friend.

Upstairs, Camilla glided into the blue room, not managing two steps in before she stopped, twirling in a circle, arms wide open. Laughing, Paige sat on the edge of the bed, allowing her friend to explore the luxurious suite which mirrored her own perfectly, although this room was a sanctuary of pale blues and creamy whites.

Finally finished with her exploration, she sat on the plush chaise that faced the large window overlooking the veranda.

"I have missed you," Camilla stated as she fell backwards. "And Chloe." As though on cue, Paige heard her loud meows as she came running into the room, heading directly for Camilla's lap. Both women laughed as Camilla stroked Chloe's soft fur, leaning in to place a kiss on the top of her head.

Shaking her head, Paige chuckled.

"She really is shameless," she declared, a warm feeling coursing through her as she observed them both. She hadn't realized how desperately she had missed her friend. She was also shaken by the feeling of extreme jealousy that had suddenly hit her when she had introduced her to Mark. Neither of them had done anything untoward, yet, witnessing their mutual appreciation of each other had elicited a feeling she was unfamiliar with. Trying to shrug it off, both women watched as Mark entered the room, a suitcase in each hand. Placing them near the larger of the two closets, he turned, his face slightly flushed.

"Camilla, I would like to thank you."

Confused, she tilted her head slightly to one side.

"Thank me?" she repeated. "Whatever for?"

Glancing towards the suitcases, he spoke, his voice teasing. "For traveling light."

Still confused, Camilla glanced at Paige, who was chuckling.

"Very funny, Mark," she replied, shaking her head slightly.

Turning to Camilla, who still had no idea what they were talking about, she explained. "He is referring to the fact that I arrived with four suitcases, which he clearly still has not gotten over."

"Oh, I have managed to get over it," Mark answered, as he placed his hand on his lower back. "But parts of me still remember."

All three laughed, and suddenly Paige felt lighter. There didn't seem to be any indication that Mark and Camilla were infatuated with each other. She only detected friendliness in their manner, although she reminded herself that she was the one who had made it clear more than once that she wouldn't date Mark. Still, she ruminated, that didn't mean she would be happy seeing him date someone else.

Confused by her errant emotions, she called out a thank you to Mark's retreating back and the two women spent the next few hours touring the home and property. Camilla fell instantly in love with Maria, as Paige knew she would. Unfortunately, Emily had to leave her position, unable to manage her classes and work. Maria insisted she could handle everything until they could find a replacement, however, both women declared they would assist her until then. They were so determined that Maria had finally thrown up her hands in surrender.

During the stable tour, Camilla found herself mesmerized by the horses. Mark had gone into town for supplies, so Adrian gave the tour, although Paige could tell that her friend's beauty had him completely besotted. Camilla noticed it as well and in true Camilla fashion, handled it with the utmost kindness.

After the tour, they made their way back to the house. Once inside, they settled in comfortably, Camilla choosing one of the large, overstuffed chairs facing the pasture. The weather was now freezing and while both women were used to winter, they both agreed that a Montana cold seemed inherently more frigid than a New York cold. Maria asked if they would like anything to drink, offering them her special hot chocolate. Both nodded enthusiastically, thanking her for her kindness.

Breathing deeply, Camilla continued to marvel at the beauty of her surroundings. After Maria brought them their drinks, which were brimming full of the most decadent hot chocolate either of them had ever had, Camilla pinned her gaze on Paige.

"How is the painting coming along?" Camilla asked, trying to appear innocent.

"Fantastic," Paige replied, suddenly fascinated with the inside of her cup.

"Yes, I have seen how 'fantastic' it is," she responded, her voice laced with humor.

"Oh alright," Paige declared. "Spit it out. What is it you really want to know?"

Pretending mock indignation, Camilla pointed to herself.

"What? Moi? I was simply asking how things were here while you have been holed up 'in the middle of nowhere' Montana with possibly the hunkiest hunk of male that I or you have ever laid eyes on. That's all I meant," she finished, picking up her cup of chocolate, sipping daintily, extending her pinky finger for effect.

Paige's unrestrained laughter spilled out, resulting in the snort that she abhorred. Shaking her head at her friend, she responded, still trying to catch her breath.

"Ok, ok," she relented. "It's really going great. He is an extraordinary artist, probably the best I have seen, and it has not escaped my attention that he is, as you say, the hunkiest hunk of man I have ever seen. I'm only too aware of that," she finished, her tone suddenly serious.

Seeing her friend's troubled expression, Camilla responded softly.

"So, you are still in the 'I will not date a client' mode, I see." Nodding, Paige remained silent.

Camilla set her cup down, then crossed her legs under her as she spoke.

"Paige, this man isn't Kyle. That relationship is long over and despite what you have told yourself, it was never wrong to have dated him. You did nothing to warrant his terrible behavior. My fear is that you aren't just unwilling to date clients, but that you are unwilling to give yourself to any man again. Ever."

Breathing in deeply, Paige rested her head against the chair, closing her eyes for a brief moment. "I'm petrified, Camilla. That it will happen again. That I will give myself to someone, that I will let them in, show the parts of me that are hidden from everyone else only to have my heart eviscerated. I don't think I could survive it twice," she whispered, her voice breaking.

Camilla felt fury rise at the devastation Kyle had left as his legacy. A single tear fell down Paige's cheek, her hand brushing it away impatiently.

"Just what exactly did that monster do to you?" Camilla asked, her expression tense.

"I told you what he did," Paige responded, shrugging.

"No," Camilla responded, a sudden realization taking hold. "No, I don't think you did."

"Please Camilla," Paige pleaded, "I really don't want to talk about this. It's just too much and I hate that I still think about it."

"It's been two years, Paige. You deserve the very best, the most incredible, amazing, loving and kind man there is, but my friend, if you cannot push past this fear, you may miss out on what is meant for you. It could be right there in front of you, and you would let it go."

"I'm sorry ladies, am I interrupting?" Mark asked as he entered the room from the back veranda. Startled, both women turned in his direction. Pointing at their cups, he smiled widely. "I see you've had the incredible honor of Maria's hot chocolate. I was never really a fan and now it's my guilty pleasure."

Glancing between the women, Mark picked up on the somber mood, quickly noting the look of abject sadness on Paige's face. Immediately, he experienced a surge of anger at whoever had dared to make her feel that way. Observing Camilla, he could see her worried expression as she, too, observed Paige, then glanced away.

Forcing enthusiasm into her voice, Camilla nodded towards her cup.

"I agree with you about the hot chocolate," she replied. "I mean it's so good it should be illegal."

Pasting a smile on her face, Paige agreed.

"It's really lovely, although I'm not surprised one bit. Maria is the best cook I have ever known."

"Yes, she is," Mark agreed, studying Paige closely. "Do you two have any plans?"

"Not today," Camilla answered. "I'm beat from the trip, but Paige mentioned going into town tomorrow." Nodding, Paige took another sip of cocoa, refusing to make eye contact with Mark.

"Well, I'm heading to the stables for a bit, to do some painting. If you need anything, feel free to interrupt." Without answering, Paige lifted her hand in a half wave as he turned, and a moment later, they watched through the windows as he walked down the back path. It had not escaped Camilla's scrutiny that from the moment Mark had entered the room, his attention had been laser focused on Paige. She didn't think he had even noticed her for the first few moments, so intent had he been on her friend. It was apparent that this man was crazy about Paige. His entire countenance softened when his eyes met hers, his concern written all over his face. How in the world her friend had not picked up on this was beyond her. She knew this was no simple attraction. Camilla felt something wonderful rise at the thought that perhaps this would be the one to love Paige the way she deserved to be.

"He cares for you," Camilla announced, breaking the strained silence. "Has anything happened between you two?"

Paige hesitated.

"A few kisses. Nothing spectacular."

"I highly doubt that if that man kissed you, it would be anything less than spectacular," Camilla commented dryly.

Paige ran her fingers through her hair impatiently.

"Ok it was wonderful. It was better than wonderful. It was beyond anything I have ever experienced before," she bellowed. "Are you satisfied?" she finished, suddenly angry. "It doesn't matter how great it was, Camilla," she continued. "He is my client. That is all he will ever be. I'm simply not brave enough for anything more," she finished, her voice now defeated.

Seeing that she was on the edge Camilla remained silent. After a few minutes she apologized.

"I'm sorry Paige," she began. "I realize you don't need me interfering in your love life so let's just drop the subject. I'm actually starving so maybe a quick sandwich and a nap before dinner later?"

Relieved, Paige agreed and soon afterwards Camilla went to her room to rest. Paige remained downstairs to help Maria prep for dinner.

Lying on the bed, Camilla was now fully convinced that her friend had feelings for Mark, more than she was willing to admit. It was going to be up to her to put some type of plan into action, although at the moment she wasn't entirely sure what the plan was. Sighing, she rolled over on her side hoping something would come to her, and quickly.

CHAPTER 9

THE NEXT FEW DAYS FLEW BY, AND PAIGE WAS IN HEAVEN HAVING Camilla visiting. She was also excited that Mark had now finished six complete canvases, more than Paige could have ever hoped for. She still hadn't seen any except for the honey-colored horse but had no doubt that they would be just as brilliant.

Mark and Adrian had offered to give them both riding lessons since neither of them had ever ridden. Paige was nervous but Camilla was ready to jump in, which was no surprise to Paige.

It was a gorgeous day and the two women chatted amicably as they made their way to the stables. As they approached, Paige's attention went immediately to Mark who was standing outside, holding the reins to a large brown horse. Paige didn't know the different names for them but this one appeared much smaller than Storm Cloud. Just as they arrived, Adrian came out leading another horse, this one slightly larger, a deep brown with white markings on his chest and head. Up close they were much bigger than Paige had expected.

Camilla was hopping from one foot to another in her excitement and Paige couldn't help but laugh at her friend's overt enthusiasm. She, on the other hand, was eying the horses warily, questioning the insanity that had led to her decision to do this at all. Mark looked ridiculously handsome as usual, Paige thought, eyeing his form-fitting jeans appreciatively. He wore a heavy flannel long sleeved shirt tucked in with a light jacket. It was a cool day, so they had all dressed warmly. As usual her heart was doing flip-flops just being around him and for some reason, she couldn't keep her eyes off his lips. Paige glanced over his shoulder, able to see the door to his makeshift art studio from her vantage point. That recollection then catapulted her to the rest of that encounter. How his hands and lips had felt on her body, how every single part of her was on fire and how badly she wanted him to do it all again, right now.

"Are you ok with that, Paige?" Jolted back from her fantasy, she realized everyone was staring at her, waiting for an answer.

"I'm sorry," she began, startled. "I'm afraid I was thinking about, umm, work stuff," she finished, embarrassed.

"I was suggesting," Mark repeated, "that we ride together for the first few times just so you can get used to the feel of the horse. Or would you rather just go solo?"

"Oh no!" Camilla shouted, causing everyone to jump, "I definitely do not want to go alone." Paige watched, incredulous, as she catapulted herself towards Adrian, grabbing his arm. "I think I'd like this horse if that works," she finished breathlessly. "You two go on that one," she finished, waving in the general direction of Mark and Paige.

"Paige, are you good with that?" Mark asked, noting the anxiety across her features. Biting her bottom lip, she eyed Camilla suspiciously before finally giving her assent. Squaring her shoulders, she replied.

"Yes, that will be fine. I'm fine. This is all perfectly fine," she repeated, still eyeing the horse unenthusiastically.

Swallowing a chuckle, Mark showed her where to place her foot when attempting to climb onto a horse but first he made her introduce herself.

"You always want to respect the animal," Mark spoke, as he lovingly ran his hand along the horse's neck. "This is Mind's Eye," he stated. "She is a Tennessee Walking Horse," he explained. "She was rescued just a month ago from a terrible situation." Paige watched as he walked to the front of Mind's Eye, whispering something to her that Paige couldn't quite hear. Glancing over at Camilla and Adrian, she saw that her friend was getting the same lesson. Finally, Mark got on, his movement one fluid motion. Paige slipped her foot off the stirrup pad three times. They weren't even riding yet and she was already acutely embarrassed.

Once she was finally up, she instinctively placed her hands on Mark's waist. It was in that exact moment that she realized the danger she had just deposited herself into. Not from the horse, although she wasn't entirely sure she wouldn't be thrown and die a horrible death, but it was the proximity to this man that posed the greatest threat. Her heart was racing, and her palms were sweaty despite the coolness of the air. Paige, hands wrapped firmly around his waist, could detect no fat beneath his jacket, only hard muscle greeted her fingers. Then suddenly they were off, crossing through an open gate into the pasture. At first, they simply trotted at a leisurely pace. Adrian and Camilla had come up beside them and Paige could see the pure rapture on her friend's face. Paige, however, was still feeling ambivalent about the experience. She was also fighting a battle within herself, trying everything she could to tamp down the passion she felt at just this simple contact with Mark. As she struggled to maintain her composure, Mark turned his head slightly.

"I'm going to give her her head," he stated. "Hang on tight and don't worry. I won't let anything happen to you," he reassured her. Paige had no idea what giving a horse their head meant but felt the sensual vibration of his words run through her. Without answering, she pushed herself even further against him. It was then that Mark lengthened the reins, giving Mind's Eye permission to run at will. At first Paige felt abject fear as the horse's hooves kicked up the earth, but within mere moments she began to understand some of the passion Mark felt for these animals. Allowing the grip of fear to slip away, Paige turned her face upwards, the whoosh of air whipping her hair chaotically. The mountaintops rushed by as they ate up the ground. It was absolutely exhilarating and ahead she could see Adrian and Camilla, her friend howling into the wind. They suddenly slowed as they approached a small stream and coming to a stop, Mark dismounted then reached up to help her off. As she slid down his body, she once again felt a rush of heat that had little to do with the sun. Stepping back quickly she avoided Mark's gaze, instead she watched as Camilla dismounted seamlessly, as though she had done it all her life. Once down she rushed over to Paige, hugging her friend tightly.

"That was incredible," she trilled, her face wreathed in a brilliant smile, eyes sparkling brilliantly.

Laughing, Paige agreed.

"I wasn't sure at first," she stated, watching as Mark made his way to the water's edge, Adrian close behind, "but I felt it as well."

"How did we never do this before?" Camilla questioned, excitement bubbling through her.

"Well, I know why I didn't," Paige answered. "We lived in the Bronx, and we were poor."

Sighing, Camilla agreed.

"Yes, I know, and well, I guess my parents were a bit too busy to be bothered with horses although," she continued playfully, "I did get plenty of lessons on how to pick out just the right pair of shoes."

Laughing, the two women walked the few steps to join Mark and Adrian.

Standing beside Mark, Paige looked up, sensing a shift within her.

"Mark, I want to thank you for today and well, for all this," she emphasized, spreading her arm wide. "I didn't think I would enjoy the whole horse-riding thing but as it turns out, I absolutely loved it. It was a wonderful opportunity and you have been so gracious. About everything," she finished, suddenly feeling shy. Mark's intense expression remained fixed on her, his eyes traveling from her eyes to her lips and back again. She immediately felt the coil of passion in her belly and instinctively stepped back.

Suddenly, Mark's expression hardened.

"You're welcome," he replied, his tone clipped. "We should head back though," he stated, staring upwards at the darkening skies. "Looks like we have a storm coming." Without saying anything further he turned, heading back to Mind's Eye. Disappointment rushed through her as she slowly followed. All four made their way back, the mood much more subdued. Paige knew she had somehow angered Mark but her frustration at the situation grew as well. She had been honest with him from the beginning, so his sullen behavior made no sense. Upon their arrival Mark and Adrian took the horses into the stables to brush them down. Feeling unsettled, Paige told Camilla she was going to wait to speak to Mark. Recognizing there was a problem Camilla nodded as she turned, making her way towards the small stream just a short distance away. Shortly afterward, Mark exited with Adrian right behind him. Seeing her, he stopped short.

"Is there something you need?" he asked politely.

"No, I'm fine," she responded, glancing nervously at Adrian. "I was wondering if I could talk to you for a few minutes?"

Adrian, sensing the tension, mumbled a quick goodbye, practically running up the path towards the house. Glancing skyward, Paige realized how black the sky had become, just as it began pouring, the rain coming down in driving sheets fueled by a strong wind. Mark pulled her into the stable and walking quickly she followed him into his studio. She noted a new canvas, distinguishable by its larger size, resting on his easel. Paige was pleased to see, too, that there were now more pieces stacked along the wall.

"Looks like we will be stuck here for a while," Mark stated as they stepped into the room. Glancing towards the small window, Paige noted the deluge of rain outside. There was a small couch against the wall to the right that Paige had not noticed before. Making her way over, she sat. Mark chose to stand, leaning casually against the door jamb.

"You wanted to talk to me," he began, his tone bored.

Irritated, Paige swallowed her anger before responding. It wouldn't solve anything if they had an argument. She was a professional, for crying out loud, known for her ability to handle temperamental clients, although, glancing over at the mountain of a man staring back at her, his expression inscrutable, she wasn't exactly sure temperamental would be the best word to describe him.

Breathing deeply, she casually folded her hands, placing them primly on her lap. Clearing her throat, she tried to ignore Mark's raised eyebrows as he looked down his stubborn nose at her.

"Mark, first I want to apologize, again, for my behavior. Truthfully, I fear I've bungled everything, and you certainly deserve better from our gallery. We pride ourselves on our impeccable professionalism, and well, she continued haltingly, I'm afraid I have allowed my personal feelings to get the better of me."

Studying her, Mark relaxed his features, as well as the rest of him.

Frankly, he was shocked at not just her apology but her admission as well. She did like him; she was attracted to him, and she was fighting it. Suddenly, Mark felt a frisson of hope. If, as she had just stated, she really had these feelings for him then perhaps he might have a chance to break down the wall of protection she had built around herself, he thought. He would be lying if he said he wasn't relieved. He was beginning to question whether he may have just imagined her interest in him. Not that he couldn't tell she wanted him, that part he knew, but what he had not been sure of was the depths of her emotions. He didn't want to just sleep with her, although his entire body was in a constant state of need, made worse by the knowledge of her incredible proximity to his bedroom. With Paige, he found himself wanting much more.

He also knew that he wouldn't be able to move to New York. His work here was too important, part of the legacy that his parents had left him. Would she be willing to give up her dream for him and did he even have the right to ask it of her, he wondered? Observing her now, dressed in jeans, sensible boots, her hair pulled back, the stray pieces that had fallen loose gently framing her face, it was difficult for him to reconcile her to the woman who had tripped out of her vehicle four months ago, high heels and all. Surprisingly, he liked them both.

After some minutes Mark finally responded.

"Apology accepted. I wasn't exactly well behaved myself," he continued, his manner contrite. "I seem to lose the better part of my reason when I'm around you." Paige didn't respond, only watched as he pushed away from the wall, closing the door as he did so.

Immediately Paige felt a rush of excitement mixed with fear. She watched as he approached, unaware that she was holding her breath. Coming down on his haunches in front of her he took her hands that had curled into fists. Slowly, he opened them, gently rubbing each palm, using small circular motions. She was drowning in his eyes, her breathing tiny gasps, as though the oxygen were being sucked from the room. She felt his fingers leave her palms, travelling slowly up her arms, then he dipped his head towards her and without thinking she pushed back. Mark, a surprised look on his face, quickly regained his equilibrium, then stood, his eyes narrowed.

Standing, Paige headed for the door. Without another word she rushed out, unable to express her sudden panic. Mark watched her rigid back as she ran out, seemingly unaware of the blinding wind and rain. He had to stop himself from going after her, something inside holding him rooted, a knowledge that she was running from her demons, not from him. Shoulders hunched in disappointment he finally turned, and removing the tarp from his latest canvas, began to paint.

CHAPTER 10

AFTER RETURNING HOME, SOAKED, PAIGE HAD BOLTED UPSTAIRS. She told Camilla she was feeling ill and hated that she was lying to her friend, however, everything in her felt raw, chaotic. She needed time to work through the plethora of emotions and although Camilla had good intentions, there were parts of herself that Paige wasn't ready to share. She had told Maria she wouldn't be down to dinner. Later in the evening Camilla had stopped in to check on her. Assuring her she would be fine, Paige sent her on her way. After a long bath she climbed into bed, emotionally spent. She lay there for over an hour, every part of her replaying what she had done in the stables. *You ran away like a coward,* she thought, afraid to be vulnerable, afraid to admit that what she felt for Mark was something primal, altogether alien to anything she had ever experienced. It was instinct to push it away, to defend herself from its tentacles.

This was not about Mark; she knew that now. Who he was continued to reveal itself to Paige, every day. His kindness, his humor, his work ethic. They had shared long conversations on the veranda rockers, where Paige was given a glimpse into the world that Mark had come from. He spoke of his parents, of their deep and abiding love one for another. Of what they taught him about the world and his responsibility in it. Paige realized that despite being raised in wealth Mark felt no sense of entitlement, in fact, he was grateful and humbled by his circumstances. As he explained it to her it simply meant that he had more opportunity to give back in some way. Paige even now felt a sense of shame when she remembered that conversation. Having been raised in poverty, Paige had been determined to have everything she felt she had been denied due to her circumstances. If she were truthful, she would have a difficult time gauging how many pairs of designer shoes she had accumulated, having designated a separate closet in her apartment just for them. Yet, aside from the grandness of his home, which, as Mark had explained, would not have been his choice, that it came with the land that he wanted, he wore no designer clothing or jewelry and drove a simple midsize truck. Every part of her knew instinctively that he wasn't Kyle. Just the thought of him brought a flash of pain and humiliation.

Suddenly Paige knew what she wanted, what she needed to do.

Glancing at her phone she saw that it was well after midnight. Getting out of bed, she slid, naked, into her robe. Not allowing herself to overthink her actions she opened her door, quickly closing it softly behind her so that she didn't wake anyone. Paige knew where Mark's room was and taking a deep breath, she glided down the hallway, arriving breathless, her excitement at war with her fear. Before she could stop herself, she turned the knob and, stealing in quickly, closed the door. It took only a few seconds for her eyes to adjust to the darkness, the moon shining through the French doors clearly illuminating the large four poster bed. She could hear his soft breathing as she approached the bed, her own coming rapidly. Suddenly she panicked. What if he didn't want her? What if he had finally figured out that she was a selfish human and was well rid of her? Then, squaring her shoulders, she allowed her robe to slide off her, landing in a cascade of silk at her feet.

Gently, she pulled back the covers, then coming up beside him on her side, she ran her fingers through his dark hair. His eyes opened suddenly, though he didn't appear startled or surprised. He simply pulled her down without speaking, his kiss hard and demanding. Gently pulling her above him, his hands quickly found her breasts, cupping them languidly. Her long hair cascaded around them as she leaned over him. Finding his neck with her tongue, she worked her way once again to his mouth. His hands ran down her back, then settled on her buttocks. His breathing was harsh, hers just as heavy. Paige knew that she should take her time, savor this moment, however, it had been too long already that her body had craved its release. Finding his hardness, she pulled him in, his sharp intake of breath followed by a guttural moan. She moved over him slowly but only for a moment, her body screaming for release. She found it quickly, Mark's own following only mere seconds later. They still had not spoken, had only come together explosively. Paige rolled off as Mark pulled her tightly against him. They remained quiet for some moments then Mark spoke, his voice husky with passion.

"Does this mean you're firing me from being your client?"

Smiling, Paige shook her head.

"I don't think that will be necessary," she replied, her voice laced with contentment. "Actually," she continued playfully, coming up on one elbow, "I think I may just have the best of both worlds."

"Oh, how is that?" he questioned, his hand reaching over to smooth pieces of hair from her face.

"Well, I have an extraordinarily talented artist and," she continued, her hand moving slowly down his stomach, curling her fingers gently around his glorious hardness, "this." Growling, he quickly flipped her onto her back, sliding into her, all hard lines and powerful muscles, moving into her as she met him thrust for thrust, waves of pleasure crashing over her. Paige had never felt so complete, a cliché, she knew, yet she had no other way to express the sense of rightness that now lived within her.

It was many hours of lovemaking before Paige reluctantly made her way back to her room. She refused to consider the possible ramifications of this evening, or of her decision. She was so dreadfully tired of worrying, and tonight, she would hold on tightly to those incredible hours with Mark. *Tomorrow*, she thought as she curled up, Chloe by her side, *would have to take care of itself.*

PAIGE WOKE UP LATE, AND SEEING THE HOUR, ERUPTED OUT OF BED. Her slightly sore muscles brought a sensual smile to her lips and after showering quickly, she made her way downstairs. Maria greeted her with a large cup of coffee which, after her first large gulp, offered her sublime pleasure. Not sure where everyone was, she decided to make her way to the stables to see if she could find Mark. Visions of last night swirled through her mind and she felt her body instantly respond.

Seeing that the stables were deserted she walked along the fence towards the smaller of the three paddocks. Storm Cloud stood facing away but turned quickly upon hearing her approach, pinning her with his incredibly intelligent blue eyes. Mark had asked that she not attempt to touch him as he was still unsure of how he would respond, especially if he were not there to supervise. Storm Cloud had not yet allowed anyone other than Mark near him. As he turned and began walking towards her, Paige backed away from the fence. He was a formidable seventeen hands high, all sleek muscle, powerful and majestic. Moving his head in a slightly up and down motion, his tail loose and swinging freely, he reached the railing, then stopped, his ears pointed forward. Unsure, Paige looked around to see if anyone was nearby. He didn't appear angry, but Paige knew nothing about horse behavior. Suddenly, he reached his head over the rail, nickering softly. Tentatively, she stepped forward, then, gently began to stroke his nose. When he moved even closer, she reached down to his neck, rubbing her hand along the corded muscle under his coat.

"Well, you're not so mean," Paige whispered quietly. "I think maybe there are just people who don't understand you," she continued. "You are in the best place in the world, Storm Cloud," she finished, a smile of joy lighting her features. Hearing his name he nickered again, the sound sending shivers down her spine. Turning his head slightly towards her, his gaze settled between the lines of her heart, leaving a permanent imprint. In that millisecond, something intangible shifted inside of her. Storm Cloud, who had no reason to trust her, had handed her his faith. Paige inherently recognized what an incredible gift had been bestowed upon her.

It was also the moment she fell head over heels in love with another rescue. First Chloe and now Storm Cloud. It occurred to her that every moment spent here drew her closer and closer and a very large part of her was terrified.

Last night had been magical, more than she could have ever dreamed. She felt the warmth spread through her as she replayed their lovemaking in her mind. Mark had been a passionate lover, yet he gave more than he took. Standing there, her hand absently caressing Storm Cloud's nose, she could see herself here forever. It both excited and terrified her. Then, a sudden feeling of dread as she realized that she and Mark lived in two completely different worlds. "I just don't see a way," she mourned, a tear sliding down her cheek. Turning, she made her way back to the house, her heart and her mind still at war.

Mark stood on his veranda; his heart lodged in his throat. He had come out to enjoy the beautiful morning when he had spied Paige standing by one of the paddocks, reaching her hand towards Storm Cloud. He had almost yelled out a warning until he realized that his horse was welcoming her attention. Aside from himself, not a single person had been able to get near him, not even his farrier. Shaking his head in wonder he relaxed, watching as she rubbed his neck. He could tell she was talking to him and something deep inside of Mark warmed, coiled. His attraction to her intensified as he observed her kindness and it only further convinced him that he wanted a future with Paige.

He didn't know how he was going to manage it, and long after she had left his bed, he had racked his brains trying to figure it out. Last night was incredible, albeit unexpected. Yet, upon seeing her there, beside him, it felt right. As though, in a way, she had come home. He knew it was a ridiculous thought, especially since he had no idea where this would lead either of them. Mark wasn't foolish enough to believe that one intimate evening spelled forever, however, he was hoping that it brought Paige a step closer to trusting him. Sighing, he watched as she began walking back towards the house, wondering where their future lay, or, if they even had one.

CHAPTER 11

Several days had passed and Paige was relieved that despite the change that her relationship with Mark had taken, there existed no awkwardness between them. It was as though they had both known this would be the natural progression, however, Paige knew that it was temporary. The logistics necessary to bring their two lives together simply were not there. Also, even though Mark had still not completed all the agreed-upon canvases, she would need to fly back to New York earlier than anticipated. There had been a young woman that Paige had hoped to convince to show her work at their gallery. The woman had finally reached out, asking to meet with Paige. Camilla was leaving in two days so Paige went ahead and booked her flight so they could travel together. Surprisingly the flight wasn't full and she was able to have them seated together.

She still hadn't told Mark, worried that he might think she had suddenly developed cold feet. If she were completely honest, she did feel like maybe they needed some distance between them. Paige wasn't ready to commit to anyone, although she refused to consider that it had anything to do with Kyle.

Early that evening, just as Paige was coming downstairs from a quick check on Chloe, Mark stepped through the front door. As usual, her heartbeat ticked up and those crazy butterflies that had taken up residence in her stomach began their winged flight. She slowly approached him, a goofy smile playing around her lips, wondering as she did so how it was that he managed to look that good all the time. As though they had been greeting this way forever Paige stepped into Mark's open arms for a warm hug. Glancing up, she met his gaze as he kissed her forehead, then stepping back, Paige asked if he had been painting.

"No," he responded as they made their way into the living room, sitting together on the couch. "Just a quick nightly check on the horses, although, I did receive a call from my friend Steve. He just got back from a stint in Europe and I invited him to dinner."

"He's the pilot, right?" Paige asked. "Isn't he the one that also rescues horses?"

"Yes, he lives not far from here. He's been gone for several weeks so I asked him to stop in."

"I look forward to meeting him," Paige replied, smiling over at him. "You have said so many wonderful things. I feel I know him." Hesitating, Paige continued. "Mark, I did want to discuss something with you, a bit off the subject."

"Oh?" Mark replied, eyebrows raised. "Anything important?"

"I'm afraid so," she answered, quietly. "I have a new client and I simply must meet with her in New York. She's flying into the city just for this consultation, so I really have no choice."

"I see," Mark replied, disbelief evident in his voice. "Are you planning on returning or may I assume this is where we say goodbye permanently?"

Paige reeled back, stunned by Mark's reaction She had never said this was goodbye forever. Clearly, he was angry, which only put Paige on the defensive.

"Mark, I never said that," she replied firmly. "Of course it isn't forever. You do remember that part of the requirement for payment is a showing of your work at the gallery? You will need to be there personally so we will see each other again."

"Oh, right. My paintings. I had almost forgotten. Yes," he continued, the hurt evident in his tone, "that would be the only reason for us to see each other."

Angry, Paige opened her mouth to respond when they were suddenly interrupted.

"There you two are," Camilla trilled, unaware that they were in a heated discussion. "I was wondering where everyone went. Whew!" she continued, flopping onto the oversized chair, "I just went for a walk and your property goes on forever," she exclaimed, addressing Mark. "How many acres do you own?" she inquired, completely oblivious to the stonelike expressions on both of their faces.

"Just over one hundred acres," Mark answered, his voice strained.

"Wow!" Camilla replied, her eyes like saucers. "I never realized it was that much." Tucking her legs underneath her, she sat further back in the chair, then, directing her question to Paige asked, "Would you two like to go out for dinner tonight? It would be great to get a little dressed up and take in the town don't you think?"

When silence greeted her question, Camilla's eyes went from one to another, the realization that something wasn't quite right finally sinking in.

"Unless you don't want to," she quickly amended, unsure what had happened between them.

"I have a friend coming over this evening for dinner so tonight wouldn't work," Mark informed her.

"Oh, sure, of course," Camilla answered, wondering how soon she could excuse herself. You could cut the tension with a knife.

Facing Mark, Paige asked, "Were you aware that Maria is off this evening? I mean, I know that you have a multitude of talents," she continued, enunciating the word talents, "however, I wasn't aware cooking was one of them."

"No, I was not aware," Mark growled, eyes narrowed.

"No, I didn't think so," Paige drawled. "So glad I could be of assistance reminding you."

Glancing towards Camilla, whose head had been ricocheting from side to side as she followed their exchange, Paige couldn't help feeling embarrassed. She was acting like a spoiled child and couldn't for the life of her figure out why this man was able to get under her skin so quickly. Catching her friend's eye, Camilla smiled nervously.

"Wouldn't it be nice if we all just went out to dinner?" she asked? "I mean it would certainly solve the problem," she finished.

Both Mark and Paige stared at her, their expressions equally mystified.

Shrugging, Camilla spoke. "It was just a suggestion. I mean, we need to eat."

Rolling his neck to release his tension, Mark stood.

"I think that's a great idea. Were all adults here, right?" he inquired, staring pointedly at Paige.

Squaring her shoulders, she responded, not attempting to hide her irritation.

"Well, some of us are, anyway," and before he could respond, Camilla stood.

"Great!" she boomed, startling Paige and Mark into silence. "Let's all meet down here at, say, seven?"

Not waiting for a reply, she grabbed Paige's elbow, guiding her to the stairs.

"Mark, we will leave the restaurant choice to you," Camilla called over her shoulder. "See you in a bit."

. . .

After Paige filled her friend in on all the details of what had been happening between herself and Mark, Camilla remained quiet.

"Do you think I'm wrong?" Paige asked, her tone incredulous. "I mean, I have a career and this is what I do. Why would he be so sensitive to that?"

"Perhaps it was just the timing," Camilla answered, her tone sympathetic. "I mean, you guys spent an intimate evening together and then boom, you tell him you're jetting off to New York. He probably finds the timing suspect," she finished, shrugging her shoulders.

"Actually, you sound like you may believe that yourself," Page responded, not attempting to keep the accusation from her voice.

"I never said that Paige, however, I do think it's a legitimate question you should be asking yourself."

Throwing her arms up, Paige expelled a sigh of frustration.

"It's just my job, nothing more. I'm sure of that."

Without speaking, Camilla stood, making her way to the door. Opening it, she turned, her gaze direct.

"Only you know for sure, Paige, and I hope what you're saying is true. That man is crazy about you and not crazy like Kyle." Seeing Paige open her mouth to speak, Camilla raised her hand, silencing whatever her friend was about to say.

"It's been two years and in two years you have not gone out on one legitimate date. You have closed yourself off from everyone except me and Paul. It's not healthy. I know you're afraid, but Paige, I have never known you to be a coward. Not ever." With that, Camilla stepped out, quietly closing the door behind her.

Paige stood frozen, trying to absorb her words. Then, sitting on the edge of the bed, she put her face into her hands and cried.

CHAPTER 12

As she stood before the full-length mirror, Paige tried to tell herself that she had chosen this outfit because she was simply tired of the jeans and sweaters she had been sporting since her arrival. The dress was a heavy black velvet, ending just above the knees. The plunging neckline was trimmed in a silver lace which also accented the long sleeves. While it caressed her body lovingly it did not suffocate it, thereby allowing it just the right amount of class. The matching bolero jacket added interest as did the black knee-high boots. Twirling, Paige found herself pleased with the result. She wore her hair up, coiled into a loose topknot, several tendrils trailing gently down her cheeks.

She was dreading the evening ahead, knowing that she needed to apologize for her behavior. Mark had deserved much more than the casual way she had informed him of her departure. It had been cowardly, a trait she was just now beginning to realize about herself. She hated it. This was not the woman she wanted to be, one frozen by fear and indecision. She was hopeful that once she returned to New York these restless feelings would subside. Distance sometimes helped perspective.

Paige also felt that she needed Paul's advice. He had helped her tremendously throughout the breakup with Kyle and perhaps he could offer her some further insight. She certainly knew how Camilla felt about it. She had made herself perfectly clear, yet Paige wasn't angry. She knew that Camilla only had her best interests at heart. As she opened the door, stooping to give Chloe one final kiss before she left, she sent up a silent plea that she didn't mess anything else up this evening. Painting a smile on her face, Paige made her way downstairs, hopeful for a peaceful dinner.

As she descended, she could hear Camilla's throaty laugh. It was the one she saved for especially handsome men. A sharp jolt of jealousy hit Paige, causing her to stumble slightly as she came down the last step. Hearing her, Mark turned. It was then that Paige realized that Mark's friend Steve was already there. As soon as Paige was introduced, she understood her friend's laugh. It hadn't been for Mark's benefit at all.

It took all her willpower not to catapult herself directly into Mark's arms. She barely noticed Steve but guessed he was good looking, in a very tall, muscular, blond kind of way. Mark, however, was elegant. Paige realized that she had never seen him dressed in anything other than jeans and work shirts. This evening he wore a pair of black dress pants that hugged his muscular thighs. The camel-colored shirt was the perfect foil for his dark hair and rugged good looks. As usual, Paige felt her body respond to his presence immediately, a hot coil of desire spiking through her belly. She was relieved when Mark ushered them all out quickly, as he had made reservations and didn't want to be late. The drive there gave Paige time to collect herself and it was then that she realized just how much Steve and Camilla seemed to like each other. Camilla had barely said two words to her, instead, she and Steve had had their heads together talking the entire drive. Paige wasn't sure if Mark was still angry. His curt nod when she had arrived downstairs had been his only greeting. Something in her had felt immediately deflated when he seemed only casually interested in her presence. It was clear now that she had indeed dressed hopeful to impress him. Mark's casual response sent a shaft of frustration through her. Paige continued to run to him and then run away. She was being desperately unfair to him and once they were all seated and had ordered, Paige made up her mind that this evening she would let him know how sorry she was. She also knew that they needed to stop any more intimacy. It had been a terrible mistake on her part. She didn't blame Mark at all. She had basically thrown herself at him. The dinner went well and she and Mark had even managed to laugh together over their horseback riding trip. Camilla and Steve added a spark of lightheartedness to the entire evening. When Paige finally made it to bed that evening, she felt much better about her decision to distance herself from Mark. Despite that, she slept fitfully, her dreams filled with visions of a certain man astride a silver stallion.

MARK STEPPED FROM THE SHOWER, HIS THICK TOWEL TIED AROUND his waist. Walking to the window he leaned against the wall, his gaze focused on the starlit sky, in awe of its spectacular beauty. Tonight, however, the view failed to dispel his frustration over his relationship with Paige, not that he was even sure they were in a relationship. Running his hand through his wet hair impatiently, he spun towards his wardrobe. Sliding it open, he chose a pair of long pajama bottoms. Once dressed, he took a book from several resting on his bedside table.

He lay on top of the coverlet, crossing his ankles as he made himself comfortable. He thumbed through the book, but the words would not come into focus, his thoughts on Paige. With the realization that he wouldn't be able to concentrate he finally gave up, flinging the book across the bed in annoyance.

The whole evening had been incredibly difficult. His attempt to tamp down what he was feeling had been arduous, however, it was his reaction when he had seen Paige in that dress that had required herculean control to disguise. He couldn't remember ever seeing anything as mesmerizing as Paige. Mark had heard the term breathtaking many times; however, it had not been until he had turned and observed her, standing there, that he had finally understood its meaning. His breath had not just been caught in his throat, he had actually swallowed it whole, his body responding so strongly that when she had approached, he couldn't even manage to speak. His emotions were at war with his reason.

He knew that Paige was still not over her previous relationship, a huge red flag, yet he couldn't help but believe that maybe she would let down her defenses enough that he could show her he had no intention of hurting her. He thought when they had spent the night together that she finally had, yet her announcement that she was leaving had dashed that hope. It had felt like a fist to the gut when she had so nonchalantly announced her departure plans. She would be headed back to New York in less than twenty-four hours, and he had no way of stopping her.

Lying back on the bed, Mark rested his forearm over his eyes. He found himself utterly frustrated with the trajectory of his relationship with Paige. He had finally found a woman whose motives were not suspect and she didn't want him. Restlessly, he kicked his feet, a wave of sadness suddenly washing over him. Ultimately, he knew he would stay true to himself. Mark had never chased a woman and he wasn't willing to start now. Sighing heavily, he turned off the light and burrowed under the covers. If it's meant to be it will happen, he decided. Finally, after an hour of tossing and turning, he fell asleep, visions of a certain woman astride a silver stallion haunting his dreams.

Paige awoke the next morning, an immediate sense of dread assailing her the moment her eyes opened. Placing her hand on her stomach she rubbed gently, trying to ease the nausea. Swinging her legs over the side she sat up, gulping in deep breaths of air aware that an anxiety attack was imminent. *No,* she thought, trying to quell the panic. *Not again.* She tried to remember the last time this had happened, hopeful that distracting her thoughts away would help to control it. Continuing to take in deep breaths, she realized it had been two years. She had been with Kyle then. Just before she had finally ended their relationship they were happening almost daily. *Why now?* she thought, perplexed. Paige remembered her doctor explaining to her that the mind worked in much the same way as the stomach. Put too much into it and it would surely come back out. *But what are you holding in?* Confused, she stood, then hearing a soft knock on the door observed Camilla peek her head in.

"May I join you?" she asked, walking in without waiting for an answer. Turning briefly, she closed the door before placing her full attention on Paige. "You look terrible," she observed, her expression one of concern. "Are you feeling alright?"

Shaking her head, Paige walked over to the large settee, sitting on the edge.

"I'm having another one of those anxiety attacks," she replied, her tone bleak. "It's been several years and I just can't understand why."

Crossing the room, Camilla sat on the bed, facing Paige.

"Well, you are obviously worried or upset about something to cause this. Is it because you're leaving tomorrow morning?"

Paige immediately felt the nausea rising. Placing her hand over her stomach she closed her eyes, inhaling sharply.

"Possibly," she finally answered, the nausea subsiding as she continued to gulp air.

"Paige, what is it you want?" Camilla asked, her voice laced with worry. "You obviously have feelings for Mark. I mean you slept with him for crying out loud," she continued. "I know you Paige, and you are not casual. There was something pretty deep driving you when you made the decision to go to his bed. You need to figure out what that was."

Tilting her head back, Paige stared at the ceiling, hoping that the answers to the universe would be written there. When she realized it was merely a plain white ceiling, she brought her head back down, meeting Camilla's eyes.

"It doesn't matter what it is," she stated, her tone determined. "I'm going back to New York. Mark will finish his work, do the show and come back here to his beautiful grand mansion and rescue many more horses after which, I am confident," she continued, her voice breaking slightly, "he will meet the woman of his dreams and settle down to make babies. Happily ever after and all that."

"I see," Camilla replied. "Well then I guess it's all settled," she continued, her tone now sarcastic. "You go back to New York, instead of facing the truth here, settle back down to your life of hiding in your oh-so-chic Manhattan apartment, never again to give a thought to the man who might just be the yin to your yang. Just like that," she continued, snapping her fingers, "you're going to hand him over to some other incredibly fortunate woman to have and to hold from this day forward. Yes, I can see why you would be confused as to why you're suffering an anxiety attack."

Paige stared blankly at Camilla. She heard the words yet even as strongly as her friend felt about her decision making, they were not enough to pierce the defenses she had built to protect herself. She knew Camilla couldn't possibly understand why her wall needed to be so high. It reached the heavens, its expanse as wide as the oceans. She had been building it since her childhood, starting when she was bullied in school for wearing second-hand clothes and shoes with holes. When her mother had died, she added yet more bricks to help her cope with her loss, and when she had met Kyle, she had placed the rest. Brick by brick by brick. But Camilla had grown up differently. Had always known who she was, where she belonged. Even in college Paige had struggled in her classes, a difficulty that further forged her belief that she was somehow less. Paige knew that she needed her job, her Manhattan apartment, her designer clothes and shoes because without all of it, she would once again be the little girl who no one could see.

Standing, Paige slowly approached Camilla. Reaching out, she hugged her tightly, grateful for her concern. Stepping back, she spoke.

"I know that you're worried about me but please Camilla, right now," she said, taking in a shaky breath, "I just need you to be there. Let me work on me. I know that I need to. I promise, I will take everything you have said into consideration."

Shaking her head, Camilla rose, making her way to the door, turning as she opened it.

"You don't owe me any consideration Paige," she said, her expression sorrowful. "No matter what you choose I will always be your friend." Hesitating, she continued. "However, you do owe Mark some explanation. I have never known you to be unkind, Paige, and I think you have been, to Mark. I hope you find time today to try to make that right." Without waiting for her reply, Camilla left, closing the door softly behind her.

CHAPTER 13

WALKING OVER TO THE WINDOW, PAIGE STARED OUT BLINDLY. SHE knew Camilla was right. Placing her hand on her stomach which was still doing flip-flops she realized that she had no right to spend a night with Mark, to give him the impression she was ready for a solid relationship. Squaring her shoulders, Paige promised herself that she would speak to him. She wasn't sure if she could entirely make the situation right but could at least try to make it better.

Paige didn't have much of an appetite and despite Maria's delicious breakfast spread, all she could manage was some toast and tea. Asking if she had seen Mark that morning, Maria informed her he had left to go into town to the feed store. Disappointed, Paige decided to head down to the stables to visit Storm Cloud. Since their first meeting, Paige had tried to sneak him a treat once a day. She didn't think Mark knew and for some reason she felt she wanted to keep it to herself. Pulling her jacket tighter against the brisk wind, Paige walked into the stable heading directly for his stall. She wasn't sure if he was there or out. Coming abreast of it she smiled when she heard his soft nickering of greeting. Opening the stall, she went in, her hand pulling out the large carrot she had confiscated from the refrigerator before heading out. As soon as Storm Cloud eyed his surprise he tossed his head in excitement. Laughing, Paige fed him the treat, rubbing his neck as he chomped away. The stall was enormous, with enough room for several horses at a time. Standing, she spoke to Storm Cloud about her current dilemma, asking for any advice he could offer. When his intelligent eyes met hers, Paige blinked. It was as if he knew the troubles of her heart, his eyes offering her what compassion he could. Shaking her head at the fanciful notion, Paige gave him a quick kiss on his nose before letting herself out. Just as she turned to head back to the house, she observed Adrian heading towards her, an angry scowl marking his features, clearly unhappy that she had been in Storm Cloud's stall. Upon reaching her, his first words confirmed that she was correct in her assumption.

"Paige, you must never go into his stall alone," Adrian stated firmly, not bothering with a good morning. "He is highly unpredictable and could be very dangerous."

Smiling her very best smile Paige replied, her eyes dancing mischievously.

"Really? You mean that horse?" she continued, looking over her shoulder at Storm Cloud.

Annoyed that Paige was not taking him seriously, Adrian stepped closer.

"I'm not sure what you have been told about Mark's horse, but he isn't one to take chances on. You know nothing about him."

Returning his direct gaze, Paige replied.

"I think I know him quite well. In fact, you could say that he and I are pretty tight." With that, Paige shifted to walk around Adrian but suddenly stumbled. Instinctively she reached for him, pushing him as she did so. He slipped backwards and within seconds they both went down, Paige landing on top of Adrian with a hard thump. Momentarily stunned, Paige took a moment to catch her breath. Glancing down her nose at Adrian, Paige found his stunned expression comical and was helpless to hold back the burst of laughter that erupted. Scrambling, she was attempting to extricate herself when she suddenly heard a deep voice booming from above her.

"I see you managed to find an interesting way to entertain yourself today," Mark drawled, his extreme irritation evident in his voice. Her giggles lodged in her throat, Paige turned slowly, still on her hands and knees, positioned over Adrian. Paige instantly recognized the worn black cowboy boots. Her eyes moved slowly up the long legs, crossing over the two bulging forearms currently placed over a broad chest, upwards still, until, impaled by his thunder and lightning eyes, which, at the moment were more like thunder, she blinked rapidly. A slight smile playing on her lips, she finally managed to get herself upright, with Adrian springing from the floor like a jackrabbit as soon as she stood. Brushing herself off, she tried to remain calm, despite the look of hostility playing across Mark's features.

"Mark, I can explain," Adrian began, attempting to remove bits of hay and dirt off his pants.

"No need," Mark answered, his gaze directed at Paige. "I'm sure you are not to blame."

Blinking furiously, his eyes dancing from Paige to Mark, Adrian nodded. As though the hounds of hell were behind him, he quickly made his way out of the stable.

"Really Mark," Paige reasoned, "there is no need for that ridiculous scowl on your face. I tripped and Adrian merely tried to stop my fall, which, well, clearly didn't work, as we did in fact fall." Feeling ridiculous, she continued brushing herself, avoiding his eyes.

"It could have happened to anyone. I mean people fall all th—"

"What were you doing in here?"

Surprised, Paige finally met his glance.

"In here?" she repeated. "You mean in the stables or—"

"Yes," he enunciated. "What were you doing in here?"

"Oh, well I needed to talk to you so I thought you might be here," she finished, squeezing her hands together nervously. "Of course I didn't. Find you, that is."

"Maria told you that I was at the feed store," he continued, pinning her with his stare. "She let me know that before I headed down here."

"She did?" she answered innocently, eyes widened in surprise. "I guess I must have forgotten," she finished, shrugging her shoulders.

"Well, you were very distracted when I found you. I can see how that would have, ahem, clouded your memory."

Squaring her shoulders, Paige stepped up to him, eyes narrowed.

"Are you implying that something untoward was happening here?"

"No, I'm not implying it, I'm stating it as a fact."

"Why you, you wretched horrible ma—"

Suddenly Mark wrapped his arms around her, pinning her against his broad chest. Before she could form a coherent thought, his lips found hers. Their mutual passion ignited ferociously. Paige knew it was wrong but was helpless to stop it. Allowing herself this one pleasure she relaxed into him. Feeling her surrender, Mark pulled her even closer, his lips slanting over hers, their tongues in an age-old duel of shared fervor. As one of his hands slid over her breast, kneading it gently, Paige moaned into his mouth. The sound ignited a raging lust in Mark and with a whoosh, Paige found herself lifted off the floor.

Carrying her into his painting room, he lifted one foot, kicking it closed. In two strides they reached the couch, Mark kneeling with her still in his arms. Their kiss had not been broken and even now, as he lay her down, following with his body, each was reluctant to end their contact.

Paige felt his need, mirrored by hers. The coiled tension in her belly trailed fire through her limbs. She wanted him, needed him, now. Pulling away slightly, Paige stared into his eyes, now a deep passion-filled purple. She pushed one hand gently against his chest shakily. Mark moved slowly off her, resting back on his heels. She saw stark disappointment cross his features.

Without speaking, her eyes locked onto his, she removed her jacket. Then, slowly, she lifted her sweater over her head, revealing a pale pink bra. She watched as Mark swallowed hard, and she could see the surprise, then the passion race across his features. Forcing herself not to overthink this moment she felt herself relax, determined to enjoy this experience with him before all courage deserted her.

Soon they had removed all their clothing, and as Mark filled her with his passion, she lifted to meet him, rocking in unison, crying out her completion seconds before his own growl of release came. It was some time before either had the strength to untangle themselves, neither speaking as they dressed, both trying to digest their lovemaking.

Finally, Mark spoke, his voice soft.

"I know that what just happened doesn't mean that you have changed your mind about us. I don't want you to feel pressured. Whatever happens moving forward," he continued, "must be mutual. It has to be right for both of us."

Relief flooded through Paige. While she held no regret for what they had both just done, she also wasn't ready for any type of commitment. *It's always wonderful in the beginning,* she thought, remembering how perfect Kyle had been in the first few months of their relationship. But then, everything had changed. Mark wasn't Kyle but her heart wasn't ready to risk everything.

Watching the myriad emotions cross Paige's features Mark felt a stab of pain when he realized that Paige was reassured by his words. Which, he pondered sadly, means she still isn't ready.

"Thank you, Mark. For understanding my need for space and time. I want you to know that what just happened here, between us, meant something. No matter what happens," she continued, fighting back tears, "it's so very important that you know that."

Unable to speak, Mark nodded his understanding. They walked back to the house together, each deep in their own thoughts.

Just before they reached the house Mark spoke, his voice laced with amusement.

"By the way, I happen to know what you were really doing down in the stables earlier."

"Do you really?" Paige queried, her own eyes blinking mischievously.

"I believe you might have been visiting a certain silver stallion and sneaking him contraband."

Laughing loudly, Paige repeated, "Contraband?"

"Absolutely," he replied, chuckling. "Don't think I haven't noticed your frequent covert trips to his stall."

On a serious note, Paige asked, "Are you comfortable with my visits to Storm Cloud? I know how much he means to you."

Reaching for the door handle, he paused.

"It isn't about my comfort. It's about him and he clearly has an affinity for you. As do I," he whispered as they stepped inside.

Nodding, Paige watched silently as he made his way upstairs to get ready for dinner. Her heart ached knowing that their goodbye in the morning could very well change everything. *You will eventually lose him,* she told herself, the thought like a punch to the gut. *If there were ever a time for you to figure yourself out, it would be now.* Later, as she packed, it was as though her arms and legs were under water, everything taking enormous effort, and Paige knew, deep in her heart, that she might never see this room, this home, Storm Cloud, Maria, ever again.

UPON HER RETURN TO NEW YORK, PAIGE LOST HERSELF IN WORK, trying desperately to put Mark far from her thoughts. Yet, no matter how late she worked, how exhausted she was, ultimately, when her head hit the pillow, she could only see him. Her thoughts were flooded with images of their lovemaking causing her own passion to ignite, leaving her feeling restless and aching with need. It had been almost three weeks and she had not spoken to him since leaving the ranch. He had left a message with Paul that he was close to finishing and Paige had felt the sting of rejection that Mark had clearly avoided speaking to her. *Why is he avoiding me?* she wondered anxiously. *We were on good terms when I left, so that can't be it.* Frustrated, she tried not to read too much into it. Camilla no longer brought up the subject and Paige was grateful. She felt raw inside, and if she were completely honest with herself, just a little bit lost as well. Her appetite had suffered as a result, and she found herself thinner than she liked. Standing naked in front of her full-length mirror one evening, she observed her body critically, cupping each breast. They too were smaller, and she couldn't help but wonder if Mark would still find her attractive. Annoyed that her thoughts had once again immediately gone to Mark, she grabbed her robe off the bed, belting it furiously. As if sensing her misery Chloe began to howl, making her way to her empty food dish. Realizing she had forgotten to feed her dinner, Paige rushed to fill the bowl, feeling guilty as she did so. *He has you so spun around you're even forgetting poor Chloe*, she thought. Making her way to the refrigerator she opened it, staring blindly inside. Nothing called out to her. Suddenly, she remembered the ice cream Camilla had brought the previous evening. Grabbing the container and a spoon she made her way to the couch. Sitting, she placed a small blanket onto her lap. Staring out at the city lights she ate spoonful after spoonful of the decadent dessert, trying to fill the void that followed her daily. Sighing, she sat quietly until the sound of her phone vibrating broke the silence. Peering over her ice cream to see who it was she froze. Kyle. This was the third call from him since she had been home. He never left a message, so Paige was left to wonder at his intentions. Suddenly angry, she grabbed it off the table. Before she could change her mind Paige answered. "What do you want Kyle?" she spat out.

After a brief hesitation, she heard him speak, his voice exactly as she remembered it, self-assured with a side of cockiness.

"Whoa!" he responded, sounding mildly shocked. "Why so angry? I just wanted to reach out, maybe catch up. We're not enemies, are we?" he finished, trying to sound friendly, although, to Paige, it sounded contrived.

"We have exactly nothing to talk about, Kyle. If it's about your upcoming showings, you know that Paul handles you exclusively."

"No, it isn't about that, Paige," he answered, attempting to sound injured. "I just miss our talks, that's all. There are no hard feelings on my end and well, I guess I was hoping you were over me by now."

"Over you?" she burst out, incredulous. Suddenly, she began to laugh. "Oh, that's rich," she continued, between chuckles. "Trust me, I have been over you for quite some time."

"Really?" he responded, his voice laced with anger. "Well, if that's true then maybe we could meet for lunch sometime. Unless," he continued, "you're afraid that some of those feelings might come back?"

Sighing, Paige responded, weariness evident in her voice.

"Kyle, I have no intention of ever having lunch, or dinner or coffee or anything with you ever again. Not today, or tomorrow or ever." Hearing his sharp intake of breath Paige quickly continued before he could speak. "And just so we are clear, it isn't because I don't trust myself with you. It's because I find you repulsive, I find you selfish, and I find you arrogant. Don't call me again, Kyle. I won't answer," and with that, she ended the call. Paige made the decision to block him, even though he was a client. *He is no longer my client,* Paige told herself. *You have no reason to ever speak to him again.*

Suddenly, she felt lighter than she had in a very long time. Turning on the television, she opted for a comedy and settled in for the evening, Chloe purring on her lap. She reminded herself of how far she had come since their breakup. It occurred to Paige that Kyle had had no effect on her senses, other than making her angry with his ludicrous accusations. These days there was only room for one man in her thoughts, she noted, and he certainly did not make her feel angry. In fact, she thought, a smile playing on her lips, a picture of Mark clear in her mind's eye, quite the opposite.

CHAPTER 14

"IT LOOKS LIKE MARK IS FINALLY FINISHED," PAUL ANNOUNCED AS he entered her office. Sitting across the desk from her, he crossed his legs casually, leaning back. Startled, Paige tried to keep the surprise from her voice.

Schooling her features, she answered, "I'm glad to hear that. I was hoping we would be able to have something by Christmas." Paul studied her, his head leaning to one side.

"He specifically asked if you could meet him at the airport. He has shipped his canvases already so we should have them soon." Feeling a sudden rush of exhilaration, Paige took a deep breath. She didn't want Paul to know how much it meant that Mark had asked for her specifically. It had taken all her resolve not to call him, feeling that to do so would only send the wrong message. She had missed him so much, seeing his smile play through her mind. Realizing that Paul was waiting for her response, she cleared her throat. Speaking nonchalantly, she leaned back, trying to appear completely relaxed.

"Of course. Have you scheduled the showing yet?" she asked, her heart rate suddenly taking off like a gazelle with a tiger behind it.

"I did. I thought December fifteenth would be perfect. We can do a two-night showing, invite all the right people and free Mark up for Christmas. I believe he mentioned he would be having guests over for the holidays so this would assure he could be back in time to prepare."

Guests? she wondered. What guests? He had not mentioned any family other than his aunt. Unless he has met someone. The thought immediately caused her stomach to drop. He was gorgeous and wonderful and kind. *Did you really believe that he has been sitting there for all these weeks just pining away for you?* she asked herself.

"Paige, are you feeling ill?" Paul asked, concern evident in his tone. "You seem off, not yourself. If you are at all uncomfortable picking Mark up I can send a driver."

"No!" she exploded, causing Paul to flinch, his eyes blinking furiously.

"I mean, no, of course not," Paige continued, her voice reverting to normal. "Mark and I have a wonderful professional rapport," she stated, almost choking on the word professional, a sudden vision of Mark kneading her breasts wreaking havoc with her self-control.

Clearly puzzled, Paul stood, not entirely believing his protégé was as unaffected by Mark as she purported to be.

"Good," he stated. "I will get his airline ticket and set him up at the usual hotel."

"Great," Paige answered, her smile forced. "Just let me know when I need to get him."

Giving her a thumbs up, she watched as Paul walked away, then slumped into her chair. Keeping her feelings about Mark a secret had been extraordinarily difficult, but more than anything she didn't want to disappoint Paul.

The debacle with Kyle had been embarrassing and although Paul insisted that she had done nothing wrong, she still carried the shame with her. She had blocked him and her former fiancé was nothing if not temperamental. Even if he had complained, Paige knew that Paul would never bring it up, cognizant of her sensitivity. Still, a part of her couldn't help but wonder if he would retaliate. *It wouldn't be the first time*, she whispered to herself.

Glancing down at her opened calendar, she realized that for Mark to have his showing before Christmas he would need to come within the next several weeks. The thought of seeing him elicited an instant coil of passion to snake through her. In her mind's eye, Paige allowed herself to remember their last time together. Immediately she felt the desire pulse through her, the strength of it surprising her. With an expansive breath she shook her head, trying to dispel the images. Frustrated by her weakness, she stood, then began pacing the room.

It had occurred to Paige on several occasions that Mark would not always be her client. She came to a sudden halt, wondering what would happen if he decided this would be his only show. Hope rose at the thought. If Mark didn't pursue his artistic endeavors, then he would no longer be her client and she would be free to continue their relationship. Still, her heart sinking, the truth was they would want Mark to continue to paint, if they could convince him, that is. It would be her job to negotiate any terms after the initial show and that would of course be based on his popularity. "He's going to be spectacular," Paige said out loud, the brief feeling of hope beginning to die. She couldn't possibly commit to him before she knew what his plan would be. It would be grossly unfair she realized, heart sinking, to him and to Paul. They both deserved better than that. Sighing loudly, she sat back down, wondering how in the world she would ever be able to remain professional with the man she believed may have irrevocably stolen her heart.

. . .

MARK RODE STORM CLOUD FOR SEVERAL MILES, GIVING HIM HIS head. The rush of cold air helped to dispel the constant images of Paige that now haunted him almost exclusively. Finally, slowing to a trot, Mark turned back towards the stable. Paul had contacted him last night with all his travel information. He would be in New York in just two days. His body instantly tightened just at the thought of being close to Paige. It had been this way since she had left and Mark felt like he was in mourning. He purposely had not called her, afraid he would say too much, knowing that she might possibly get spooked. Still, as he closed in on the stables, he felt that he must tell her what he was feeling. The idea that the only thing keeping them apart was a crazy sense of responsibility to Paul and Roja Galleries was infuriating. He refused to believe that it was because she still had feelings for her ex-fiancé. Mark had watched her expression the few times the subject had come up and he was positive she was finished with him. Arriving back, Adrian grabbed the reins as Mark dismounted.

"Can you give him a good rub down?" Mark asked, rubbing his hand along Storm Cloud's nose.

"No problem," Adrian replied enthusiastically. Mark smiled, noting the excitement on Adrian's face as he walked Storm Cloud back to his stall. Turning, he headed back to the house, his eyes on the dark clouds rolling in. He hoped the weather stayed clear enough for him to fly out. Winter storms in Montana could be fierce. Entering the kitchen, he inhaled deeply, the smell of Maria's fresh apple pie wafting deliciously throughout the house. Seeing her at the counter Mark stopped, then, pulling out a stool sat facing her. Turning, Maria smiled broadly.

"I have some hot stew for lunch if you're hungry," she informed him, wiping her hands on her apron.

"Hmmm," he replied, glancing towards the oven. "I kind of have my mind set on that pie," he answered. Laughing, Maria walked towards him.

"It still not quite ready," she told him. "Plus, you cannot have pie for lunch. It isn't healthy," she finished good naturedly, wagging her finger at him. Smiling, Mark couldn't help the warm rush he felt at her concern. Losing his mother at such a young age had forced him to grow up quickly and that included carrying a great deal of responsibility on his young shoulders. To be mothered by Maria felt wonderful, though he would never in a million years admit it.

"Ok, ok, you win," he replied, hands up in the air as if to surrender. "I will have some stew, but I insist on two slices of pie as a reward."

"Deal!" she crowed loudly, as she scooped a bowl full of the stew from the pot simmering on the stove. After getting him a drink, some fresh baked bread and his utensils she sighed with satisfaction as she watched him take his first bite. Noting her anxious stare, Mark pretended to be thinking about whether he liked it, then, sensing her concern he laughed.

"Maria, it's wonderful!" he exclaimed, feeling guilty when he saw her relieved expression.

"I'm sorry Maria," he apologized. I was teasing.

"Oh psssh," she replied, waving her hand. "I knew it was good all the time." Laughing, Mark dug in, finishing in record time as Maria cleaned the kitchen. They had hired another assistant, but she wouldn't be able to start for several weeks. Mark was worried that Maria was doing too much but she insisted it was perfectly manageable. Still, he had insisted on giving her a substantial raise, so substantial that she had begun crying, adamant that it was too much. Mark knew that her husband had not worked in sometime due to a health issue. Maria not only cared for him but her aging parents as well. He wanted to make her life easier, feeling that he was able to do so for a reason. His parents had always been exceedingly generous, and Mark was as well.

"Maria," Mark began, watching her as she removed the apple pie, his mouth beginning to water just looking at it. "I will be leaving for New York in two days and will be gone for close to a week," he advised. "Do you need anything before I leave?"

"No, I have everything I need," she replied. "More than everything," she finished, smiling widely. "Good," Mark replied. "There's plenty in the household account but I didn't want to forget anything."

"Are you going to bring Paige back here where she belongs?" she asked, her eyes innocently gazing back at him.

Stunned, Mark just stared back at her, his eyes blinking furiously.

"I— well, if— I'm not—"

"Well, of course you are!" she trilled, clapping her hands happily. "You love her and she loves you. Goodness," she continued, "anyone with a half an ounce of sense can see that when you are together. Like a magnet to steel," she finished, completely ignoring the fact that Mark had been rendered speechless.

Then, shoulders relaxing, Mark sucked in a large gulp of air. Letting it out in one whoosh, he answered.

"I'm sure going to try, Maria. I'm going to give it all I have." Until that moment, when he spoke the words out loud to someone other than himself, Mark hadn't realized that that was his plan all along. He didn't care about the show, although he did want the money for the animal relief fund. He was astounded that the work he did was deemed worthy of so much. Maria was right. He loved her. He loved Paige.

Nodding, Maria turned. Cutting a piece of warm pie, she placed it in front of him.

"Good. It's a rare thing to find love. It's something you should fight for."

Digging into the best apple pie he had ever had, Mark agreed. He wasn't just going to New York to show his artwork. He was going to bring Paige back. He was going to bring her home.

CHAPTER 15

PAIGE STOOD IN THE BAGGAGE CLAIMS AREA, HER EYES STRAINING through the throng of people approaching. She had come close to asking Paul to pick Mark up himself since she was a complete bundle of nerves, however, that would require explaining to her boss why she was a bundle of nerves to begin with. He would certainly have questions for her if she attempted to get out of it. Her bedroom at home looked like a cyclone had gone through it as she had pulled one outfit after another from her closet, finding fault with all of them. Finally, she had settled on a fitted pair of gray wool pants with a luxurious white cardigan. Paige had opted for the only pair of black boots she owned that were not stilettos. She didn't feel brave enough to take on Mark and walk in heels through snow drifts.

Suddenly she spied him, his shoulders well above the rest of the travelers and her heart slammed into her throat. She watched him approach, cognizant of the multitude of admiring glances from every single female he passed being tossed his way. Every inch of her on fire just from the sight of him. His face broke into a wide smile when he spotted her, inducing a gentle warmth to envelop her. Then he was standing before her, all hard lines and beautiful eyes, smelling like fresh air and kindness and without any thought she walked right into his arms. It was as natural as breathing, as she became enfolded in all his strength. With Mark, she felt more. Stepping back reluctantly, she immediately mourned the loss of his warmth. She also couldn't seem to stop smiling no matter how hard she tried.

"Well, if I had known I was getting that kind of welcome I would have been here much sooner," he said, his voice low and husky, sending shivers through her.

"Well didn't I mention that's one of the perks of choosing our gallery?" she quipped as they made their way to the turnstile.

"No, I don't think you did," he replied, pretending to ponder the question. "I'm sure I would have remembered that," his tone suggestive. Once again Paige felt a frisson of excitement run through her.

Laughing, she watched as he grabbed his suitcase, then turning, he began to walk away. Confused, she fell into step, while simultaneously looking back over her shoulder

"Is that all the luggage you have?" she asked, her expression perplexed.

"It sure is. I pack light. You said I only needed two dressy outfits so that's in here and the rest is what I wear every day, plus extra pairs of clean underwear," he finished, winking at her outrageously.

Stumbling, Paige felt a burst of pleasure race up her arm when Mark grabbed her elbow to help steady her while she tried to recover from the extreme sexiness of this man.

For his part, Mark appeared as cool as a cucumber. Falling into step once again she became aware of an extraordinarily beautiful young brunette staring with unabashed appreciation at Mark. Narrowing her eyes, Paige linked her arm through his, sliding in closer to his side. Glancing up at him, it was immediately clear that Mark had no idea or simply didn't care about his effect on the opposite sex. Something inside suddenly relaxed and Paige once again marveled at the incredible man of character that Mark was. She couldn't help but be excited that she would have him all to herself for the next few days. Mark had been disappointed that his aunt would be out of state visiting a sick friend, so aside from the show there would be few distractions.

THE DRIVE TO THE HOTEL WAS PURE TORTURE FOR MARK. THE moment Paige had come into view, it had taken every ounce of self-control to stop himself from getting down on one knee and asking her to marry him right there and then. She was the sexiest woman alive and sitting next to her in the taxi he quietly inhaled the scent of her. Feeling himself relax, he glanced over at Paige. She had her hair pulled back in a sleek ponytail. He could see the pulse in her slim neck move along with her heartbeat. He wanted to run his tongue along its length, then slowly make his way to her mouth. She wasn't wearing lipstick and he liked that. Her lips were perfect without anything and just full enough. Feeling his body's quick response to his lustful musings, he pulled himself back. Looking for anything to distract himself, he asked about the hotel he would be staying at.

"Oh, I think you will love it," she told him, nodding enthusiastically. "It's actually a suite, which as you know, in New York, is hard to come by but we want only the best for our clients," she finished, breathlessly. Paige had been picturing him naked at the same moment that he asked about his hotel. Nodding, he smiled, though to Paige it appeared forced. She knew that he had to be exhausted from the long flight.

"There is room service at the hotel," she informed him, "in case you're hungry."

"Actually, I'm not," he replied, holding back a yawn. "I think the trip is catching up however," he admitted sheepishly. "I had some new rescues come in from out of state so I didn't get much sleep last evening."

"Oh no need to apologize at all. Tonight, just get caught up on rest and tomorrow I will pick you up to take you to the gallery for a tour."

"Thank you. I really look forward to meeting Paul. He knew my parents," he added, just as they pulled up to the hotel.

Paige didn't respond as they exited the vehicle. She waited while he got his suitcase then, assuring the taxi driver would wait, she walked with Mark inside. It only took a few moments to get his reservation settled. Turning, she looked up, noting how tired he looked.

"Mark, you need to go right to bed," she said sternly, grabbing his elbow while she steered him towards the elevator. Handing him his room key, she pressed the elevator button.

"You know," he said, leaning sideways so that he spoke close to her ear, "I'm not too tired for company in case you would like to come up," he whispered seductively.

Her body responding instantly, Paige turned her head so that their lips almost met. She could feel his hot breath when suddenly the elevator doors opened. They both moved apart quickly.

"I think tonight," Paige asserted, "you need to sleep," gently pushing him into the waiting elevator. Stepping in reluctantly, Mark gave her a hungry look. Everything in her wanted to throw caution to the wind and go with him. Still, she knew it would be wrong.

"Goodnight," she whispered under her breath, watching until the doors had closed completely. Turning, she made her way out, getting back into the waiting taxi. When she finally arrived home, she felt completely drained from the encounter. Later, lying in bed staring at the ceiling, she tried to find a resolution to her predicament, but nothing seemed right. *Still*, she thought, even as she was falling asleep, *there must be a way. You must find a way.*

. . .

THE NEXT DAY PAIGE AWOKE TO A GLOOMY SKY, DARK CLOUDS threatening another snowstorm. Breathing deeply, she tried to stem the tide of butterflies in her stomach. Mark was here, the image of him bringing a smile to her lips. She felt lighter and happier just knowing he was close, that she would see him later. A rush of warmth enveloped her. Immediately her thoughts went to a way that she could be with Mark permanently, assuming that was he wanted that as well. Drumming her finger lightly along her chin she spoke into the room. "Do something, Paige. You cannot continue with one foot in and one out. You're going to have a pick a side and if it isn't with him, then be prepared to move on without him."

Last night had yielded her no new solutions to her emotional dilemma. There were moments when she wanted to jump into the deep end but too there were moments when she skidded to a stop at the very edge of the water. Mark was the deep end and Paige knew that he was an all or nothing guy. It made her wonder if she was an all or nothing girl. She stood in her closet, tossing outfit after outfit aside. Finally, she settled on a clingy wool dress with a matching jacket. Studying her shoe and boot collection, Paige suddenly felt a weariness steal over her. "Why do you have so many shoes?" she announced to the closet. She hadn't worn many of them in several years but there they sat, collecting dust. "Like your heart," she whispered. Hearing her front door open followed by Camilla's greeting she turned, smiling as her friend walked in, carrying her favorite cappuccino.

"I come bearing gifts," she reported, placing the cup on the bedside table. Taking in the chaos, she sat on the edge of the bed, swinging her booted foot lightly. As soon as Chloe heard her, she came out from her plush bed, jumping onto Camilla's lap. Then, spinning several times she curled herself into a ball.

"She does like you better," Paige complained, her eyes furrowed in mock annoyance.

Peering over her coffee cup Camilla smiled, then took a

careful sip of the steaming brew. Swallowing, she blinked her wide eyes innocently.

"I do not concur," she answered. "I believe she loves us both equally."

"Well considering I'm the one that feeds and houses her I should command more than fifty percent of her allegiance."

Laughing, Camilla nodded.

"Good point."

Coming right to the point Camilla asked, "So, did you see Mark last night?'"

Closing her eyes briefly, Paige sighed heavily.

"I did. In fact, I was the one who picked him up from the airport and then dropped him off at his hotel."

"'Dropped him off?" Camilla questioned, tilting her head slightly.

"Yes, dropped him off as in, I didn't go up to his room as in, nothing happened."

"Did you want something to happen?"

"Actually Camilla, yes. The truth is I could barely keep my hands off him, I wanted to catapult myself onto him, kiss him absolutely everywhere but, in true Paige fashion, I did exactly none of that." she finished, trying desperately to hold back her tears.

Gently extricating Chloe from her lap, Camilla placed her cup on the dresser before taking her friend into her arms, holding her gently. It was all that Paige needed to finally let everything out. Everything she had been repressing, burying, finally rose, pouring itself out of her eyes. The tears ran unchecked down her cheeks until finally, the sobs ended, replaced by quiet hiccups. Exhausted, Paige finally stepped back. Making her way to her vanity, she pulled tissues impatiently

"You are obviously crazy for this man and frankly I don't blame you. He's amazing, Paige."

"Yes, he is," she replied. "He is amazing, and he's sweet, kind and generous. He is all of that and so much more."

Suddenly it was as though the largest lightbulb in all the world switched on.

"I love him, Camilla," she whispered, the wonder of that realization lighting her features. "I love him." Spinning in a circle, her arms opened wide, she sang loudly to the room, "I love Mark Richards!"

Laughing, Camilla observed the sheer joy on her friend's face. She felt tears slide down her cheeks, so relieved that her friend had finally pushed through her fear.

"So, what is the next step? Will you tell him today?"

Shaking her head, Paige continued dressing while she spoke.

"No, I'm going to tell him after the final show. I don't want to jeopardize his success in any way. Also, he will still be my client until then."

"But won't he still be your client after the show?" Camilla questioned; her expression perplexed.

"No, he won't be, because I plan on resigning my position with the gallery."

Stunned, Camilla could only stare at her friend, her expression one of pure shock.

"I'm sorry, you're going to do what?" Camilla sputtered, unable to fully comprehend what her friend was saying.

"It just came to me," Paige responded, her tone completely confident. "It's the only answer. This way I don't jeopardize his relationship with the gallery. I know that he will be a huge success, Camilla. I'm not wrong about that. His talent extends far beyond any other artists I have known. It's rare and precious and the world needs the beauty that Mark will bring to it through his works. I don't ever want to get in the way of that, but, at the same time, I can't let him go. I can't have both, and if I can't have both, then I choose Mark," she finished softly. "I choose love."

"Does it really have to be all or nothing though?" she asked.

"This is the career you chose because you love it. Mark wouldn't want you to give that up for him."

"But I'm not. That's just it. I do love my job, I love art of all forms, I love the beauty that it brings to the world. I can still love all that, Camilla. I'm not losing anything. In fact," she continued softly, "I will gain so much. For so long I have placed my career, my apartment, my 'things' above everything and yes, everyone else. I truly believed that without all of this," expanding her arms to encompass the room, "I was nothing."

At Camilla's sharp intake of breath, Paige paused.

"How could you have ever believed that?" Camilla exclaimed, her expression sorrowful.

"I just became lost, spinning in circles, completely unraveling, until I met Mark. He doesn't see my career, or my designer clothes, or my oh-so-chic uptown apartment," she explained, smiling. "He sees me," she emphasized, pointing to herself. "The me that's been buried inside, the me that somehow convinced myself that my worth was in what I did, what I wore, where I lived, instead of the me that could care less about all of it. The me that would willingly live under a bridge with the most incredible man in the world and still know that I hit the jackpot." Taking a breath, she sighed softly. "He opened his heart, left himself vulnerable, for me. So you see," she marveled, "I am still unraveling, but tenderly, wholly, and with all of my heart."

Eyes bright with unshed tears, Camilla hugged her friend tightly.

"I'm with you all the way Paige," she sniffed. "I always have been, and I always will be."

"Now finish getting dressed and go get your man!"

Happier than she had ever been, Paige complied, her plan for 'getting her man' already forming. *Ready or not, Mark,* she mused, *here I come.*

CHAPTER 16

Mark's frustration was palpable. He had been trying to get Paige alone for several days yet there always seemed to be copious amounts of people surrounding them constantly. Paige had been pleasant and irritatingly professional the entire time he had been here. It was almost as though she were purposely avoiding him and it was grating on his nerves. Tonight was the final showing and he was glad it was almost over. He felt out of his element here even though New York had once been his home. He missed the beauty of Montana, he missed his bed, he missed Maria's cooking and he most especially missed Storm Cloud.

The opening night exhibition of his work had sent excited ripples throughout the art community. His work had met with considerable accolades from some of the most famous art critics in the world. Already they were clamoring for more, yet all Mark could think about was Paige and trying to get her alone so he could share his feelings for her. Every time he thought he had her pinned down she would be off once again, leaving him exasperated. Glancing around the crowded gallery he finally caught sight of her through the crush of people. She was wearing a deep red velvet dress that did nothing to hide her curves. As Mark made his way towards her, two things stood out. One, she was spilling out of the dress and as much as he appreciated the vision, he didn't approve of the way the man she was conversing with was ogling her. He could tell by her pained expression that she was uncomfortable, and he couldn't be sure, but she appeared apprehensive as well. Secondly, as he walked up to them both, was how incredibly in love with her he was. Coming to stand beside them, Mark searched her face. She smiled brightly, yet Mark could see that it did not reach her eyes. In fact, she looked taut, as though she were balancing on a tightrope. Shifting his attention to the stranger standing in front of Paige, Mark immediately disliked him. His perfectly groomed hair along with his obviously contrived insouciance instantly put him off, not to mention the way he continued to undress Paige with his eyes.

"Who is your friend?" Mark asked, his eyes locked on the peacock in front of him.

"I'm sorry, of course," Paige responded, her voice anxious. "Mark this is Kyle. He is an artist as well and one of Roja's clients."

"Kyle," Mark said, fully understanding now why Paige was so nervous. "Oh yes," Mark drawled, ignoring Kyle's outstretched hand. "I have heard some, ahem, things about you," he finished, his expression murderous.

Reeling backwards, Kyle's eyes narrowed, instantly recognizing Mark as an adversary.

"I'm quite sure you have," he replied, thrusting his thin chest forward. "For instance, perhaps you have heard that my first showing netted three times the buyers that your tired animal paintings did."

Without waiting for Mark's reply, he continued, smiling maliciously. "And of course, you must be very aware of just how far back Paige and I go," he challenged, purposely casting a look of lust in her direction.

Closing the distance between them, Mark looked down his

nose at the man who had hurt Paige. "Just so we are clear," Mark growled, his eyes narrowed in anger, "she is a woman who is to be respected. If you ever," he enunciated, "ever look or speak to her again in the manner that I just witnessed I will tear you limb from limb." Kyle's eyes widened; fear etched across his features. "Do you understand me?"

Nodding furiously, Kyle bowed slightly in Paige's direction before spinning on his heel, heading directly for the door. They both watched as he quickly made his departure. Afraid to look at Paige, Mark continued to look at the now empty doorway until he heard what he thought was a snort. Turning, he noticed that Paige's shoulders were shaking. Terrified that he had upset her he was just about to apologize when she looked up at him.

"That was absolutely incredible," she chortled, laughing so hard that she couldn't speak for a few more seconds. Relief flooded through Mark.

"I was afraid you were angry," he stated, his face wreathed in humor.

"Angry? Oh no," she beamed. "It was priceless. I don't think anyone has ever spoken to him that way, although, they really should have," she finished, casting him a grateful look. "Thank you, Mark. No one has ever stood up for me the way you just did and well, it meant so much to me."

"Paige," Mark began, curling his fingers around her wrist. "There's something I need to ask you."

A sudden look of panic crossing her features, Paige abruptly pulled her hands away.

"Not now Mark. I'm so very sorry," she apologized, as she once again began to drift into the crowd. "Let's meet up at say 11:00 over by the stairs," she directed, pointing in that general direction. "We can have dinner together if you would like?"

Breathing out a sigh of frustration at once again losing sight of his quarry, he nodded his acquiescence. Watching as she moved through the crowd, he told himself that he just needed to be patient. Glancing at his watch he muttered under his breath. "Two hours." He could do it. Two hours to hold the girl of his dreams, hopefully, forever.

THE NEXT FEW HOURS DRAGGED AS MARK MADE SMALL TALK WITH complete strangers. He was grateful, of course, for the opportunity and most especially for the money for the animal relief fund, however, these types of social gatherings were tedious. Grabbing at his necktie he tugged on it, attempting to loosen it so that he could breathe. He was quite surprised that he hadn't face-planted due to oxygen deprivation. Still, the room was finally beginning to clear out and the evening came to a much-anticipated end. He had lost sight of Paige and when he glanced around the room she was nowhere to be found. He knew that the offices were on the second floor, so he decided to go up. He couldn't wait another minute to make her his. Once he reached the top of the stairs, he spied several offices to his left and veered off in that direction. As he approached the first door, he saw that it was slightly ajar. Hearing Paige's voice he stopped, realizing she was speaking to someone. Not sure he should interrupt, he stood frozen. Suddenly he heard an upraised voice. Mark recognized it as Paul Roja but couldn't understand why he sounded so upset. Not wishing to eavesdrop but equally concerned for Paige, he waited a moment then heard her speak.

"Paul, I need you to accept this letter of resignation," she pleaded, desperation evident in her tone. "I don't feel comfortable working with Mark under these circumstances. It isn't his fault," she continued. "It's just how I feel, and I desperately need you to understand that."

The force of her words knocked Mark backwards. It was as though every bit of oxygen had suddenly been siphoned from the atmosphere. Panicked that she might discover he had heard her, he spun, quickly making his way downstairs then outside.

Standing on the sidewalk he gulped in large amounts of frigid air, trying to absorb the pain that racked him. Observing a waiting taxi, he quickly jumped in, giving his hotel address. Mark was stunned at just how wrong he had been, still reeling from the blow. She didn't want him. Leaning further back in the cab, Mark ran his hand through his hair impatiently. He was determined to make things easy on Paige, by going back home tonight. She would never need to see him again. Once he had made up his mind, Mark quickly packed and managed a seat on a redeye leaving in just a few hours. He packed quickly, angrily shoving his clothes into his suitcase.

Later, on his flight back, Mark played everything back again, feeling the wound open each time he heard her words. It occurred to him that he had just been paid a million dollars and it had come with a broken heart.

PAIGE SPENT THE EVENING TRYING TO FIND MARK. IN A PANIC, SHE had enlisted the help of Paul and Camilla, neither of whom could understand what had happened. The hotel attendant finally told them that Mark had checked out and had asked the taxi driver to take him to the airport. She had tried calling him repeatedly, but it just went straight to voicemail. Everything had been going perfectly so she was utterly confused by his behavior. He had been attentive, loving and had defended her to Kyle. Paige knew she could not have mistaken the look in his eyes. It was real, it was love, or so she had thought. Paige was unable to sleep all night, worrying. Maybe there had been an emergency? But he would have told her surely before leaving? No goodbye, just gone. Paige felt all her old hurts come to the surface and couldn't help but wonder what she had done that was so very terrible. He was too good to be true, she told herself. Part of her, the part that still felt the pain of rejection, the pain of poverty, the pain of self-esteem that had been shredded, felt she deserved it. She couldn't

help but wonder if he had simply realized that he wanted something more than what she could offer. It left her with a crippling
sense of loss, one that she knew would haunt her.

After tossing and turning most of the evening, Paige finally
got out of bed. Making her way to the living room she sat on the
couch, her thick blanket wrapped around her and watched the
sun rise. The tears came and she let them. She knew better than
anyone that life didn't always work out the way you thought, and
this was just another one of those misfires, she thought bleakly.
She was madly in love with a man that didn't love her back. It
was that simple and that cruel.

Long after the sun came up Paige lay there, Chloe by her side,
crying until she couldn't cry anymore. Her phone had been
buzzing with calls, but none were Mark, so she ignored them all.
She wasn't ready to talk about what she was feeling. The pain was
so raw, so new, she needed time to absorb it all. Even the briefest
notion of a life without Mark was more than she could bear so
instead, she forced herself to focus on everything and anything
else.

Still in her pajamas, she began cleaning out her closet,
throwing everything into large plastic trash bags. Paige wanted to
donate as much as possible. In that moment she realized it had
given her momentary pleasure but not true happiness. She sat in
the middle of her closet, surrounded by more shirts and dresses
and shoes than she could wear in two years. Paige felt another
wave of pain slice through her, and the tears began anew. She
wondered how it was possible that she could still cry, incredulous over the human body's ability to produce what appeared to
be a never-ending supply of tears. Bowing her head to her chest
she wept, and it was there that Camilla found her.

Concerned when she didn't answer her phone, she had rushed
over. Now, seeing her, Camilla felt a wave of compassion. Bending, she placed her arms around her friend and held her, feeling
her slim shoulders tremble with the weight of her agony. Paige

rested into her, remembering a time once before when her friend held her, as she spilled her grief.

Joining her on the floor, Camilla sat across from Paige waiting for her to regain her composure. Her friend looked terrible she noted, folding her hands as she waited patiently to hear what had caused Paige so much anguish.

Camilla had tried calling Mark several times, but it kept going to voicemail. Finally, she managed to track down Maria's number. Mark had provided it to Paul as an emergency contact. Following a brief conversation, Camilla remained as confused as ever. Mark had arrived home safely according to Maria, however, he looked haggard to the point that Maria was frightened for him. He had insisted he was fine and given direct orders that he would only speak with Paul, no one else. When Camilla asked if he had mentioned Paige, she became quiet.

"He did but I'm afraid it wasn't good," she informed her sadly. "He simply said that Paige was too opportunistic for his taste and asked that I refrain from trying to elicit any further information regarding 'that woman.'"

"Opportunistic?" Camilla exclaimed. "That simply isn't true, Maria. I know that for a fact."

"I don't believe it either, but it doesn't matter what you and I believe, Camilla. Mark is convinced that Paige does not care for him. He is a proud man. In this instance, I'm afraid I cannot help any further," she finished, her voice forlorn.

"Thank you, Maria, for everything. I understand your position. Please, if anything changes, call me immediately. I will always be available for you, day or night."

"I will Camilla, and please, tell Paige how very sorry that it has come to this. Such a disappointing ending."

Now, as Camilla observed her broken friend, she decided to keep her conversation with Maria to herself. It would only confuse the situation further and open an already gaping wound.

Paige finally found the strength to leave her closet, even

managing to shower and eat some soup. She still didn't want to talk about Mark, preferring to hold her pain close. It was an altogether familiar hurt, one that she knew well. Camilla stayed until close to midnight when Paige finally convinced her that she would be fine.

"He's out of my life and that is something I need to accept," Paige said, shrugging her shoulders. "The fact that I may never know why is moot. I will survive," she assured Camilla. Still, after she was gone, Paige felt the despair rise once again and wondered if she would ever know true happiness. "Why, Mark?" she whispered to the New York skyline. "Why?"

CHAPTER 17

ADRIAN AND STEVE STOOD AGAINST THE PADDOCK RAIL WATCHING Mark work Storm Cloud. It had been a month since his exhibition, and he still refused to reveal what had caused his abrupt departure from New York or his refusal to discuss Paige at all. Steve had tried several times to get him to talk it out, only to be warned that should he continue to bring her up, he would be asked to leave. It was clear to everyone how much pain he was in. He had known Mark for many years but not this driven, angry version. Scrutinizing him as he worked Storm Cloud, Steve could see the lines of exhaustion etched across his features. He often worked well into the evening hours. Still, all he could do was hope that whatever demons drove Mark would soon depart. He wasn't sure how much longer his friend could continue this way. He and Camilla were in touch often, both worried about their respective friends. Like Mark, Paige refused to discuss her feelings, although when Camilla had shared with Steve what had happened in New York he was just as puzzled as she was. Something happened but unless Mark was willing to speak about it, and he had made it abundantly clear he was not, then all they could do was wait it out.

. . .

MARK TRIED TO HIDE HIS IRRITATION AS HE BROUGHT STORM Cloud to a halt before dismounting. Steve was a close friend but these days Mark felt like he had turned into a babysitter. It was beginning to grate on his nerves. Seeing him now with Adrian caused a spark of frustration as he knew Steve was here only to check on his mental health, which Mark knew was perfectly fine. He wished they would all just leave him alone. Since returning from New York, Mark had thrown himself into myriad new projects including taking on four new rescues. Adrian had become invaluable and along with Maria helped keep everything running smoothly. His unwillingness to discuss Paige was self-preservation. It even hurt to hear her name. He greeted Steve, then walked Storm Cloud into his stall, feeling her ghost follow him inside. Even as he engaged in small talk with Steve she was there, always on the fringes. He went through the motions, doing his chores, eating his meals, and riding his horses. The truth was he didn't feel alive, didn't feel whole. Paige had managed to get in, all the way in, he realized, to a place he had never known existed before her. Still, life went on and Mark knew that he had people and animals depending on him.

Paige had tried calling him for several days after his departure and then the calls stopped. It had been a relief as he wasn't sure how much longer he could have gone without hearing her voice. He had been tempted on many occasions to call her, to ask her why she had felt the need to string him along when she had no real intention of being in a real relationship. He had given her his heart and she had broken it. It was worse at night, when he couldn't escape from the memories. He could see her, smell her, feel himself inside of her. Night after night he was tormented and wondered if he would ever fully heal. As he walked with Adrian and Steve back towards the house for lunch, he could see her, standing at the window, waving, her beautiful smile beckoning.

He knew he still loved her, aware that in the month that he had neither seen nor spoken to her, his feelings had not diminished. The pain belonged to him and he was not willing to share it. Mark knew he was too raw, still trying to navigate the void she had left. To speak the words out loud seemed too permanent. So, he pretended he was better, that his life was moving forward even though, deep down, he was aware that his family and friends knew better. Paige still very much held his heart, pain at the realization slicing through him. She still had him and he was afraid that she always would.

PAIGE STEPPED OUT OF THE TAXI ONTO THE BUSY SIDEWALK, pulling her jacket tighter against the brisk New York wind. Most days she preferred to walk home from the gallery, finding it helped with her mindset although today the weather was just too cold. Walking quickly towards the large glass doors, she stepped over several large piles of slush before entering her building. Glancing down she was glad she had purchased more sensible boots. They were both warm and adorable. The best part was she had acquired them from a discount shoe store in Queens. Lately she had been cognizant of her exorbitant spending habits, preferring to put the extra savings towards some amazing charitable organizations. She refused to consider why she had suddenly had a change of heart, satisfied that it had simply been a matter of coming to the realization on her own.

Christmas had been bleak, although Camilla and Paul had tried to keep her busy. She had accepted several invitations to holiday parties only to find that she wanted to leave as soon as she arrived. There were several new artists that had joined the gallery, each keeping Paige busy with their upcoming exhibitions. Mark's showing had netted the gallery much more than Paige had paid out, as she had known that it would. She had buyers clamoring for more of his work, however, Paige had turned over all further business in that regard to Paul. Even now she was unable to look at any of his pieces. While she no longer spent hours crying, she was unable to break free of the love she held in her heart. She had long since given up on trying to keep him from her thoughts. Instead, she chose to remember the moments that she cherished, the laughter, the beauty of their lovemaking, the stories they shared with each other under a starry Montana sky.

While she didn't understand why Mark felt the way that he did, she realized it no longer mattered. Kyle had taught her that she deserved the very best and Paige no longer felt inclined to settle, aware that she wanted it all. She let herself into her apartment, divesting her jacket and boots in the hallway before making her way to the kitchen. Starting a cup of tea she grabbed Chloe up into her arms, nuzzling her soft neck. Her welcoming purrs eased Paige's bruised heart. The one thing that she was sure of was that she now fully understood Mark's passion for rescues. Settling down in her favorite sweats, her hot tea on the table beside her, Chloe snuggled on her lap, she realized that rescuing worked both ways.

Paige remembered how Mark's features softened whenever he was with Storm Cloud, how his shoulders relaxed, the gentleness in his touch. She could see his love and as she tenderly stroked Chloe's softness, she knew without a doubt that their rescues rescued them right back. Staring out at the darkening sky Paige wondered what Mark was doing and if he ever thought of her at all. *I hate that you are absent from me, Mark,* she whispered into the room.

THE NEXT MORNING PAIGE AWOKE TO THE SOUND OF HER PHONE vibrating on the bedside table. Grabbing it she saw that it was Camilla.

"Good morning," she answered sleepily. "What are you doing up—"

"Paige, I have some bad news," she interrupted, her voice troubled. "It's about Mark." Her heart slammed into her throat while her hands began to tremble, a bolt of adrenaline coursing through her body. Sitting bolt upright, she swung her legs over the side of the bed. "What's wrong?" she asked anxiously.

"It's Storm Cloud. He's ill, very ill I'm afraid. Mark is beside himself. Hasn't left his stall in two days."

"Oh no!" Paige whispered, devastated by the news. "Poor Mark."

"Wait, how did you know about this?" Paige asked, confused. "Did Mark call you?"

"Well, no not exactly," Camilla replied. "Steve told me."

"Steve told you?" she repeated. "Why would Steve tell you?"

"We have been in contact, you know, occasionally. Anyway," she continued impatiently, "what are you going to do?'"

"I'm hanging up and then I'm booking a flight."

"You are?" she asked incredulously.

"Yes, I am," Paige declared, determination in her voice. Hopping out of bed, she threw open her closet door grabbing a suitcase off the shelf.

"Can I do anything to help?"

"Could you take care of Chloe? I don't know how long I will be gone but I can't take her this time."

"Of course I will," Camilla reassured her.

"And Paige," Camilla offered, "for what it's worth, I think you're doing the right thing. I'm proud of you."

Closing her eyes, Paige fought her tears. She thought of Storm Cloud and how very much she loved and missed him. That alone was enough to propel her towards her decision to return immediately but she also knew that Mark was hurting. He was hurting and her instinct to be there to comfort him, overriding her abject fear of his possible rejection.

After she hung up, she quickly called the airlines, managing to get a flight out at midnight. Paige finished packing then called Paul and explained what was happening. The night of the exhibition he had refused her resignation, finally convincing her that she could still handle the clients from Montana. It might mean a few more flights every few months but it was workable, he had insisted. Paige had thrown her arms around him, kissing his cheek soundly, then raced out to find Mark to beg him to marry her, but he had already left. Funny how suddenly none of that mattered. She wasn't going to let pride stop her from doing what she knew was right. Storm Cloud meant everything to Mark and she realized as she headed to the airport that he meant more to her than she had thought. *Whether they know it or not, they need me and I'm going.*

Mark leaned his head against the stall, stretching his legs out in front of him. Every part of his body hurt. He ran his hand through his hair, then rubbed the back of his neck, trying to ease the headache that had plagued him since Storm Cloud had become ill. He watched him where he lay, his eyes closed, his breathing labored. Steve and Adrian had stayed in the stables with him, Maria bringing them food and hot drinks. The viral infection was rare and the vet had done all that he could. It was up to Storm Cloud now. He had set up a makeshift bed with some thick blankets and a pillow. Realizing how late it was, he made himself get up and move to the other side of the stall. Yawning, he checked Storm Cloud's breathing again before closing his eyes. His condition had been the same for several days and Mark was scared to death. There was something extraordinary about their relationship, he realized, as he lay staring at his friend. Something that most wouldn't understand

and for which Mark himself had not the words to explain. He only knew that he wasn't going to leave him.

Settling in, he finally found sleep, and dreamt once again, as he did every night, of a beautiful blonde woman astride a magnificent silver stallion.

PAIGE ARRIVED AT THE RANCH THE NEXT MORNING AT ELEVEN. SHE was exhausted and more frightened than ever but still determined to offer her help. When Maria opened the door, her eyes had widened in surprise, then she drew Paige in, hugging her tightly.

"I knew you would come," she whispered as she stepped back. Smiling tremulously, Paige looked quickly around.

"Is Mark with Storm Cloud?" she asked, placing her suitcase by the door.

"Yes, I'm afraid he hasn't left his side, poor man," she replied, biting her lower lip.

"How is Storm Cloud?" Paige asked, a feeling of dread heavy in her chest.

"The same," Maria replied sadly. "No change."

"I was so hoping for better news." Glancing towards the windows, Paige felt a familiar sensation in the pit of her stomach, a clenching sensation. Whenever she was afraid to do something, it would come like this, hard and fast. *Push through the fear,* she told herself. *There's no turning back.*

"Do you mind if I leave this here?" she asked, pointing to her suitcase.

"Oh, I can bring it up to your old room," Maria answered, grabbing the handle.

"You may want to wait," Paige told her, her manner hesitant. "I'm not exactly sure if Mark will consider me to be a welcome guest," she said, her expression worried.

"Psshhhh," Maria replied, waving her hand. "That man will be ecstatic to see you. Just go down there and tell him you are stay-ing, don't ask. I have a feeling you may be surprised at your reception," she finished, her lips lifting in a knowing smile.

Squaring her shoulders, Paige walked slowly down the path towards the stables, her legs like lead. She felt flushed even though there was a brisk frigid wind, whipping her hatless hair. Her gloved hands were clenched into fists which she had shoved into her jacket pockets. Paige desperately wanted to run towards him yet desperately wanted to run away too, she realized just as she walked into the stable. Ahead, she could see Adrian, leaning against the stall door. Hearing her approach, he looked over, a slow smile spreading along his features. Meeting her halfway he hugged her hard, then stepping back, Paige smiled at the grati-tude she read in his eyes.

"Where is he?" she asked though she knew he would be in Storm Cloud's stall. Pointing his thumb over his shoulder Adrian smiled, though his expression was marked with worry.

"See if you can convince him to sleep in his own bed tonight. He only leaves to take a shower, change and then he's right back with him." Nodding, she began walking slowly towards the stall, unbuttoning her jacket as she did so. Despite the icy air she was suddenly sweating. Before placing her hand on the latch, she removed her gloves, tucking them in her jacket pocket. Glancing at Adrian, he gave her a reassuring thumbs up. Squaring her shoulders once again, she opened the gate. Her eyes immediately found Storm Cloud, who was centered in the stall, lying on his side. Something in the vulnerability of his position pierced her heart and she took a deep breath to stem the pain. Her last image of this fierce stallion was at odds with the creature who now labored to breathe. Then her eyes rested on Mark, sound asleep beneath a pile of pillows, his head facing Storm Cloud's. She could see the dark circles resting beneath his thick eyelashes and she was sure he had given up shaving entirely. His beard was full and thick, although it only seemed to enhance his already rugged good looks.

Quietly she made her way to him, bending, as she sat gingerly beside him. Reaching over, she gently brushed away the hair that lay over his forehead. It, too, had grown longer. Suddenly he growled low in his throat, then lay on his back, placing his forearm over his eyes. Turning she looked at Storm Cloud. His eyes were closed, his breathing shallow. She placed her hand gently on his cheek, rubbing it back and forth softly. He opened his eyes, a spark of recognition briefly lighting them. Then he nickered lightly, his way of welcoming her. Tears coursed down her cheeks and she let them. It was a hurt like no other, one that stole her breath, that she wanted to run from but could not. No matter the outcome, she would stay by his side. Raising her eyes to the ceiling she whispered, "please, please let him have a happily ever after." Scanning the stall, she spied another blanket tossed in the opposite corner. Rising, she retrieved it, wrapping it closely around herself, then, making her way back to Mark she lay down beside him, her back against his side and within moments, exhausted from the flight, fell fast asleep.

CHAPTER 18

A FEATHERY TOUCH ALONG HER CHEEK WOKE PAIGE. OPENING HER eyes, she could see Storm Cloud. Noting that he was still breathing she relaxed, relief flooding her. Only then did it occur to her that it was Mark touching her. Slowly she came to a sitting position before turning fully to face him. He was leaning against the stall, his expression assessing. It took every ounce of self-control she had not to launch herself into his arms.

"Why are you here, Paige?" he asked quietly, his eyes full of pain.

Clearing her throat before she spoke, Paige sucked in extra oxygen for sustenance.

"I heard about Storm Cloud and it was just instinct. I know what he means to you and, well, what he means to me." Glancing quickly over her shoulder, she sent the beautiful stallion a smile, then turning back to Mark, whispered, "I couldn't imagine not being here."

"So, you came all the way from New York for Storm Cloud?" he asked in disbelief. "Or maybe," he continued, his features hard-ening, "you came to see if I could make you and your gallery more money. Believe me, Paul has already received my answer and if he was banking on you again, he was sorely mistaken."

Paige felt the sting of his words, flinching as the painful barbs found their mark.

"Mark," she began, her body beginning to tremble. "It wasn't just for Storm Cloud; in that you are correct." Seeing his satisfied expression, she hurried on. "But you're very wrong about the painting. I don't care if you ever paint again, although it would be a shame with your level of talent." Staring straight into his eyes, now clouded with doubt, she asked. "Why did you leave, Mark? I thought, I believed," she enunciated, "that we felt something for each other. I couldn't have imagined that could I?"

Barking out a short laugh, he cocked his head to one side.

"Are you seriously telling me that you have feelings," pointing to his chest, "for me? Because that isn't what I heard you say."

Confused, Paige shook her head.

"What I said?" she repeated. "I don't understand."

"I heard you, Paige. I heard you tell Paul that you couldn't work with me for another minute or something to that effect," he spit out. "You wanted to be away from me so badly, in fact, that you told him you were going to resign, just to avoid me."

Paige felt the shock of his words race through her body. Desperately she thought back to that evening, trying to remember what she had said to Paul, then, snapping her head back, she realized Mark must have overheard them talking.

Suddenly, she was furious. More furious than she could ever remember feeling.

"Why you stubborn, self-righteous, ridiculous man!" she raged, shooting him a withering stare as she jumped to her feet. "Were you eavesdropping on my private conversation with Paul?"

Standing as well, Mark folded his arms defiantly.

"I went upstairs to find you," he defended himself, and heard raised voices. "I was concerned," he laughed bitterly, "so I stood for a moment and that," he continued with an angry glare, "is when I heard what you said," he finished sarcastically.

"I see," she bit out, crossing her arms as well. "Did it ever occur to you that you might just have taken what you heard out of context as most people who eavesdrop so often do?" Before he could respond, she stepped forward, pointing her index finger at his chest furiously. "Do you have any idea what pain you have caused me?"

"Caused you?" he bellowed. "Caused you?" his eyes flinging shards of lightning at her upturned face. "I'm the one who was mistreated here, I'm the one who had his heart ripped out."

Chest heaving, Paige tried desperately to stem the tears that threatened to fall. Swallowing convulsively, she blinked hard several times, trying to control her breathing.

Closing her eyes briefly, she stepped back. Calm, her voice now firm and steady, she spoke.

"For your information Mr. Richards, I went upstairs to resign my position, that much is true. However, what you completely misconstrued was why. I was resigning because that evening, that amazing evening I was going to get down on one knee and command you to marry me." Observing his look of astonishment, she rushed on. "Yes, it's true. I didn't feel it was right to continue as curator knowing that I wanted a future with you. I was desperately afraid to make another mistake, so I decided to resign," she whispered, heartbreak visible in her eyes, "so that I could be with you. Because I couldn't imagine my life without you in it," she finished, sadly. "Not for a job, or an apartment, or clothes and certainly not for money. You should have come to me, Mark, but instead, you ran away."

Mark stood rooted, a feeling of dread ricocheting through his body. Gazing at her now, he could see the suffering that he had stupidly visited upon her, the pain he had unwittingly caused the woman he loved as well as himself.

Then, suddenly, a burst of overwhelming joy followed by a

wave of relief swept aside everything else as the realization that Paige loved him finally began to sink in. This extraordinary woman loved him. Then, the enormity of what he had done hit him like a tidal wave, pushing him back against the wall.

"Paige, I—" extending his palms forward, "I don't know what to say. I was an idiot; I made a terrible mistake. Please believe me. I am so madly, so deeply, so completely in love with you but on reflection, I know that I allowed my previous relationship to overshadow my good sense. I guess it was easier for me to believe that you didn't want me than to believe that someone as incredible as you could possibly love me. Please," he whispered earnestly, "please tell me that it isn't too late."

Paige allowed herself to slowly absorb Mark's words. He had hurt her terribly. In order to move forward she would need to decide. Whether to trust what he was saying, a risk, or turn away forever. Smiling, she felt the answer as both relief, then elation wrapped themselves around her bruised heart. Mark loved her back. In her there existed acceptance that he was human, as was she. Imperfect at best. His eyes caressed every part of her, and in their depths, they revealed the truth.

"Mark," she whispered as she walked into his arms, "we have been so foolish." Resting her head against his chest, she closed her eyes, listening to the beats of his heart, reassuringly slow and steady, relishing the warmth of his arms as he pulled her tightly against him. From somewhere above her head, she heard him speak, the low rumble in his chest offering a sweet caress to her cheek.

"I will never let you go, Paige. I want all of you, forever." Stepping away, she tilted her head back, her response shining from her eyes. She watched, mesmerized as his lips came down on hers, a feathery whisper at first, his breath warm. Impatient, she rose on her tiptoes, curling her fingers into his hair as she pulled his head hard against her. His tongue instantly met hers, slick and altogether incredibly sexy. She marveled at the bubbles of happiness that were racing through her. Suddenly, a loud rustling sound erupted behind her. Startled, they broke apart abruptly, turning their attention to Storm Cloud. He was standing, his head tossing up and down. Rushing to him, Mark ran his hands over him, starting at his nose then along his neck and flanks. Paige could see that they were trembling as he examined him closely, his expression tense. She watched as his shoulders sagged in relief, her own breath coming out in a sigh she hadn't realized she was holding. Coming to stand in front of him, Mark looked into Storm Cloud's eyes. The two stood this way for some moments, then Mark stepped into him, his arms going around the horse's neck. Paige was spellbound, observing Storm Cloud accept Mark's embrace, even resting his head on Mark's shoulder for a moment, as if to give him further reassurance that he was better. It was a singularly profound moment, a privilege to have witnessed, she thought, goosebumps rising along her arms. Paige stood back, allowing them their space, aware of the incredible love they had for one another. Mark turned towards her, his eyes radiating gratitude. Beckoning her over, she quickly joined them, taking her time with this incredible stallion as she too, absorbed the miracle of his recovery. She had a sense, standing there, just the three of them, that she was finally free of the bonds of the past. They stood together for some time, acknowledging the sanctity of this experience and with it the unbreakable bond that had been forged. She was finally home and ready for whatever their lives might bring, armed with the love of this remarkable man and his astonishing horse.

Later that evening there was a celebration. Maria went all out preparing an incredible meal. Adrian and Steve joined them, along with Carl Reed, the veterinarian Mark hired to care for all his horses. He had called him immediately to verify that Storm Cloud was indeed on the mend. After a very thorough work-up, he had given a much-appreciated thumbs up. Sitting back in her chair, Paige placed her hand on her stomach, in awe of how much food she had just consumed, happily, eyeing the apple pie. Shaking her head, she decided that would need to wait. At least for a few more minutes.

Satisfied, she listened to the cheerful banter, allowing herself the luxury of basking in her newfound happiness. When she thought of how unreasonably they had both behaved she couldn't help but wonder at their eventual reconciliation. Pride, she knew, had almost cost them both a beautiful future. As frightening as that scenario was, Paige was also cognizant of the lesson it had taught her. Glancing at Mark, she reveled in his laughter, as Adrian told yet another joke. He was carefree, his elation palpable. Catching her eye, he winked slowly, his expression revealing the promise of the evening ahead. Paige shifted in her chair as the heat instantaneously coiled, wrapping itself around all of her. She saw his knowing smile and was amused to observe him move restlessly as well. There had been no time to talk about their future, but Paige was content to allow their relationship to evolve at its own pace.

AS MARK TOOK A SIP OF WATER, HE TRIED TO CONTROL THE ABJECT lust that Paige elicited in him. When he had woken to see her curled up beside him, he was determined that no matter what, he would try to win her. Seeing her, curled up, wrapped in a dirty blanket, he had felt his defenses slip. No longer angry, he realized that pride had its place, but for him, not when it came to his love for her. Still, he needed to know there was a chance. Closing his eyes briefly, he again felt the shock of her words, the same sickening sensation in the pit of his belly as he realized once again how close he had come to losing her forever. Looking around the table he was suddenly impatient for the evening to end. He needed to be alone with her, to touch her everywhere, as much to satisfy his love as to convince himself that she was real. That she loved him. That she would stay. Watching her now, as she rose to help Maria clear the table, he again counted himself the luckiest man alive that she had forgiven him. So intent was he on his ruminations he almost didn't catch what Carl had just shared about Storm Cloud.

"Craziest thing I've ever seen," he heard him finish.

"What was the craziest thing?" Mark repeated. "I'm sorry, what were you saying about Storm Cloud?" Glancing over at Mark he said, "I was just saying that I'm rather stumped as to his quick recovery."

"You don't think he still may be ill, do you," Mark asked, suddenly feeling anxious.

"No, no, nothing at all like that," he quickly assured him. "It's just, well, my initial thought was that he had a virus although the bloodwork was normal. In fact, all his tests were normal. I just assumed it had to be something not seen in the blood." Scratching his head, he continued. "But, now I'm not so sure, especially given the circumstances of his, ahem, miraculous recovery."

"I don't get it, Carl," Mark interrupted, shaking his head, his expression mystified. "What exactly are you suggesting?"

"I know this is going to sound crazy," and here he hesitated, quickly glancing around the table, "but if I didn't know better, I would say he was pretending to be sick."

The silence that followed his statement was deafening, confusion and disbelief evident as they all tried to absorb his words.

Standing at the kitchen counter alongside Maria, Paige almost laughed at the look of astonishment on Mark's face. He opened and closed his mouth several times before he finally responded.

"That's impossible," he stated firmly, shaking his head emphatically. "I mean, that would suggest that he had some reason to do so, which would suggest, well, that he thought about it, that it was premeditated. It's crazy," he finished, still shaking his head. Then, spreading his hands, he continued.

"Assuming its true, what would his reason have been?" Laughing, he sat back, folding his arms across his chest. "Just preposterous."

"Impossible, you say?" Maria suddenly responded. "Impossible? Of course it's possible. Miracles happen every day. Storm Cloud is incredibly intelligent," she continued, pointing to Mark. "You have said as much yourself many times."

"Well yes, but this—"

"I say he certainly could have pretended. I myself have had many pets who pretended all the time," she insisted. "So impossible?" she finished, shaking her head. "I think not."

"But Maria," Paige countered, coming to Mark's defense, "why in the world would he have done it? I mean, Chloe has pretended as well but there was a reason. You know," she continued, "like when she pretends to be starving ten minutes after I feed her. Her motivation, of course, is that she wants more food."

Both Adrian and Steve nodded their agreement. "She's right, doc," Adrian addressed Carl. "Assuming what you are suggesting is even possible, what did Storm Cloud have to gain?" Before he could respond, Maria interrupted.

"Oh, for goodness' sake!" she exclaimed, throwing the dish towel on the counter as she came to stand by the table. Placing her hands on her hips she stood over Mark, a look of annoyance crossing her features.

"He did it for you," she announced with conviction.

"Me? But why—"

"That horse knew darn well how Paige felt about you and you about her and how he felt about you both. Animals have feelings, and I truly believe, a soul. So, getting sick was a sure way to get her to come back here. Which she did," nodding in Paige's direction "resulting in your reconciliation. Which, upon witnessing, was all Storm Cloud needed to end the ruse. Good grief," she finished, waving her hand impatiently, "it's so obvious." Mumbling under her breath, she returned to the kitchen, then picking up a clean dish rag, began wiping down the stove, clearly unaffected by their stunned reactions.

For a few moments silence reigned, then, clearing his throat, Carl rose.

"Well," he announced, "I think I'm going to head home. Thank you for the meal, Maria," he stated as he grabbed his hat off the living room chair. Turning, he shook Mark's hand. "Whatever the reason, I'm most happy for you, son, and for Storm Cloud." Nodding, Mark walked him to the door. "I'll check in with you tomorrow for a report on his condition," Carl stated. With a final wave, he left, Mark closing the door quietly behind him.

Returning, Mark smiled widely at Paige, his expression leaving little doubt to his thoughts. Sensing they had overstayed their welcome, Adrian and Steve made a hasty exit as did Maria, yawning loudly as she made her way to her room. Taking Paige's hand Mark led her to the couch, pulling her down beside him. Curling her legs under her, she leaned into his side, placing her head on his shoulder. Her sigh of contentment caused Mark to chuckle. "Happy?" he asked, kissing the top of her head.

"Mmmmmm, so very happy," she answered, snuggling even closer. They both sat in silence for some time, watching the flames from the fireplace cast flickers of light that danced along the darkened room. Paige stared into the blaze, mesmerized, as she listened to the occasional crack of the dying twigs. She wanted to pinch herself, but worried that Mark would think she was crazy. Turning her head sideways, she observed him as he too was pulled into the magic of the burning light. Trembling slightly, Mark pulled her closer in response and she smiled. Fascinated by the beat of the pulse in his neck, she leaned up, gently licking it. She heard his sharp intake of breath as he turned his head to meet her lips. It was no gentle kiss. It demanded everything. Impatient, it made itself known in the power it wielded. Paige felt the shift, knew this would bring them both to a different ending than before. The kiss awakened in her heart a fierce desire to let go of every lie she had ever told herself. That she was unworthy, that she was somehow less, that her career or clothes or home in any way defined her. That was the lie she told herself as she leaned completely into Mark, her desire spiking through her in jolts of electric pleasure. Suddenly, he pulled away, his eyes a rolling storm on the horizon, its flashes of lightning caressing her. Paige read his need, his features stark with hunger.

"We need to go upstairs now," he growled, pulling her up, then rushing her towards the stairs. Laughing, Paige ran up the stairs, Mark behind her, touching her playfully as they moved quickly along the hallway, then they were in his bedroom and he was slamming the door shut with his foot. Breathless, Paige stood still as he stalked across the room towards her, more powerful than she had ever seen him. Part of her felt a tiny pulse of doubt; not that she wouldn't be enough, she knew that she was enough, only, this time, she wanted to be more. For him. For them.

Lifting her eyes to his, every reservation she might still have harbored died. There was no mistaking the love or the passion that spilled from them, and her own feelings, she knew, reflected the same. Without taking his eyes from hers, his hands slowly begin to draw her sweater up. As it rose, she lifted her arms, feeling it slide over her head. With trembling hands, she unbuttoned his shirt, impatient to feel his flesh under her fingers. She drew in a ragged breath as he shrugged it off then, she was done with waiting, done with hiding her need. She snaked her hands around his neck, pulling him to her, hearing his moan of pleasure just before his lips consumed hers. Soon they were on the bed; their clothes being tossed in a frenzy of passion to every corner of the room. Paige almost laughed when she heard one of Mark's boots hit the wall, but, as he climbed over her, all muscle and lust, her humor was quickly replaced by her own need.

She opened herself wide to him, without reservation. Then,

closing her eyes, she raised her hips, taking full control and he let her.

Paige felt his first thrust and she rose to meet it, relishing the rhythm of their need. Opening her eyes, she observed his passion etched along his features, his own eyes closed as he fought to maintain control. Then, she came apart, everything shattering into thousands of prisms of pleasure, enveloping her until she almost cried with the happiness it left behind as the first spasms faded. Mark's head was thrown back as she watched, fascinated by the muscles straining against his neck and shoulders as his own pleasure burst from him, his howl of pleasure rising to the ceiling before finally, quietly, coming to rest. Sliding off her, he pulled her against him, his breathing still heavy. She gloried in the feathery kisses he brushed along her cheek and forehead. He held her possessively, a firm, loving promise as his hands moved over her hip. They lay like that for some time, content to be in each other's arms. Then she felt him shift and resting on one elbow he smiled down at her.

"Paige, I'm going to say something, and I don't want you to interrupt until I'm finished. Can you do that?" he asked, planting a kiss on the tip of her nose. Nodding yes, she remained quiet, waiting. Clearing his throat, he locked his eyes to hers.

"First, I want to be clear that I'm not saying this just because we—well—because we—"

"Made love," she interrupted, then, noting his humorous impatience, quickly apologized. Placing her finger on her closed lips, she made a motion of zipping it, smiling innocently.

"Yes, exactly," he replied, chuckling. "Also," he continued, "there is no need for you to respond should you not wish to. That part is important," he emphasized.

Nodding her understanding, Paige waited, curious now as to what he was leading up to.

She hoped he would hurry though, her gaze taking in his bare chest. There was no doubt that as soon as he finished, she planned on catapulting herself directly onto his oh-so-manly form.

"I love you, Paige. I think I fell in love with you that first day we met. I don't know if it was when your shoe got stuck in the mud, or when I heard you curse like a sailor under your breath or the moment I first looked into your incredible eyes and in their depths, recognized a friend. I felt like I just had a gut punch and it hasn't changed with time." Reaching her hand to his face, she lovingly caressed his cheek, then placed her hand back down. Smiling, he continued.

"I want you to know that your suitcase is over by my closet," he revealed, moving his head slightly in that direction, "because this room is ours. I want you in my bed, our bed, from now on."

Paige wondered how long she could stay conscious without breathing because everything had stopped as soon as she heard him say he loved her. It was a moment that literally took her breath away, a term she had never understood until now. Blinking, she continued to stare, unable to trust herself to speak. She realized that Mark was anxiously waiting for her response. Suddenly, she sat up, the blanket falling to her waist. She saw Mark's eyes dip down, lighting up with appreciation before quickly moving back to her face, his expression uncertain.

"Mark," she began, her voice trembling slightly, "before I respond I need you to know something."

Pushing himself up to a sitting position he nodded as he faced her.

"I want you to know that I love you beyond reason. That I have from the moment I spotted you leaning against the pillar on the front veranda and asked myself how in the world I was going to represent myself professionally when you looked good enough to eat." Pausing, she could see the happiness radiating from his eyes as he chuckled. Pulling in a deep breath, she continued.

"'I don't know if I fell in love with you when you tried to proposition me, or if I fell in love with you when you refused to paint for our gallery, or," she continued softly, "if I fell in love when I observed your incredible kindness, your extraordinary generosity and knew, when I looked into the stormy skies of your eyes, that you too were a friend. I only know," she finished, moving slowly over him, gently pushing him into the soft pillow, "that I love you and I have every intention of showing you just how much." Leaning down, she met his lips with every part of her, nothing held back, no reservations, no fear. Just the knowledge that she would forever be beside this man.

CHAPTER 19

Much later, after they had a late-night snack, sitting cross legged on the bed after they had visited the stables to check on Storm Cloud, who was as good as new, they lay once again together, in their room, Paige, on her side, watching the steady rise and fall of Mark's chest as he slept, in awe of her happiness. Finally, lying on her back, she closed her eyes, reflecting on this incredible day. Tomorrow and the next day and the next she would wake up beside the man she loved beyond reason. Sliding her hand up her arm, she pinched it gently, smiling into the darkness when she felt the sting. Finally, she gently drifted to sleep, at peace, wholly and irrevocably, with herself.

The news that she and Mark were in love and an official couple came as a surprise to exactly no one. Steve had slapped him on the back, told him it had taken long enough and picked her up in a bear hug, twirling her in a circle. Maria just smiled knowingly and set about to prepare a celebratory feast. Camilla had shrieked so loudly and enthusiastically that Paige had to hold her phone away from her. Altogether, it had been wonderful to be surrounded by so many who loved and cared for them both. Paul was like a father, congratulating her, his voice filled with emotion.

"I knew he was the right one," he told her when she had called him the following day. "He will make you happy and you deserve that." His words had brought her to tears. Growing up with no father, Paul had become the closest thing she had, and she truly cherished his place in her life. However, business did go on and Paige had to let Mark know that she did have clients she needed to meet with in New York.

"I understand," he told her, pulling her towards him. "When do you have to leave?" he asked, leaning down to nuzzle her neck.

Feeling his tongue flick beneath her ear she shivered with desire. "Umm, I—well—"

Turning her head, she met his lips and was unable to form any thought whatsoever. Breaking the kiss, his expression left her with no doubt as to his intentions and picking her up, he slung her over his shoulder as he raced upstairs to their bedroom. Landing on the bed. Paige had tears of laughter rolling down her cheeks. Falling gently on top of her, Mark braced himself as he leaned in, his kiss fiery. Fueled by her own need, Paige barely remembered undressing before she was atop him, her hands resting on his chest as she took him inside of her. Her hair fell around them, as his hands cupped her breasts. Finally, they met their mutual climax, the sounds of their lovemaking slowly ebbing into silent contentment. Facing each other, Mark reached over, gently sliding a stray hair from Page's eyes. Smiling, she sighed with pleasure, doing the same for him.

"I guess we can try this again," Mark said, chuckling. "When is it that you need to leave?"

Giggling, Paige leaned forward, placing a light kiss on his lips.

"I must be back by next Saturday. That gives us a whole

week," she replied. "I hate that I have to leave so soon though," she finished, pushing out her bottom lip slightly.

"Me too. I was hoping you could road trip with me to pick up a new horse. It's about a day's drive but I can't get him before next Sunday."

"Oh no Mark! I wish there was a way to get out of it but I'm afraid I've committed." she finished sadly.

"Well, it can't be helped and believe me there will be other trips," he reassured her.

"Still," she finished, her own disappointment evident. "It would have been our first trip together as a couple."

Grinning, he pulled her against him, his need evident despite the short time that had elapsed.

"I can think of other things we can do as a couple," he teased, running his hand along her back, then cupping her buttock gently.

"Is that right?" Paige whispered huskily before her own need silenced her.

LATER, MARK LAY BACK, HIS HANDS UNDER HIS HEAD, STARING AT the ceiling. He could hear Paige's gentle breathing as she slept, his own mind racing. There was only one week left to put his plan into action. Glancing over, he smiled wickedly. He knew she would never see it coming. It had required a substantial amount of planning and the promise of secrecy from a great many people. There was always the chance that someone might let it slip, but he was banking on all his well laid plans coming to fruition. There wasn't anything he wouldn't do for this woman and Mark knew that he was more than fortunate to have garnered her forgiveness. Hopefully, she would see that every piece of him was anxious to begin their future together. With that, he finally closed his eyes and joined Paige in blissful sleep.

. . .

THE NEXT WEEK FLEW BY AS PAIGE ACQUAINTED HERSELF WITH THE day-to-day operations of the ranch. She and Mark had not discussed the future beyond admitting their love for each other. Still, Paige wondered what their next step would be. Mark had made it clear that when she didn't need to be in New York, he wanted her there with him, which she was more than happy to do. As she raked out one of the stalls, she paused, reflecting for a moment on how much had changed in such a short time. A month ago, she was lost and hurt, afraid that she would never see Mark again and now, as she looked around the stable, here she stood, in this beautiful place, cleaning up horse droppings with enthusiasm. Smiling to herself, she had just begun to rake again when she heard Adrian calling her name. Puzzled, she peeked her head out. Standing just outside the stable doors, he was frantically waving her over. Placing the rake against the wall, she blew an errant strand of hair from her eyes while brushing straw from her pants. As she approached, she could see Steve and Maria standing alongside the white plank fence. Completely confused, she walked out just as Camilla stepped out of the house, making her way down the path towards them. Clapping her hand over her mouth, Paige was dumbstruck. Camilla was supposed to be in New York right now. In fact, she had just confirmed all her flight information with her two nights ago since she would be picking her up from the airport. *What in the world is going on?* Paige wondered, watching as Camilla blew her a kiss, joining Steve, Maria and Adrian, all of whom were now standing by the fence.

Just as she was about to join them, still utterly lost, she suddenly heard the thunder of hooves. Placing her hand to her forehead to block the sun's rays, she watched as Mark, riding Storm Cloud, raced across the expanse of pasture, bits of dirt flying as the horse's hooves kicked up the earth. He told her that morning that he would be gone most of the day getting supplies. Glancing at her watch she realized he had been gone for only a few hours which did little to explain why he was now racing towards her, on Storm Cloud, carrying flowers. Unable to stop smiling, she slowly walked to the fence as he brought Storm Cloud to a stop in front of her. Automatically Paige reached out her hand to rub the horse's nose, laughing when he nibbled her hand, something he did only to her. She watched as Mark dismounted, then, handing her the flowers, he leaned across the fence to kiss her.

"What are you doing, you insane man?" she whispered, unable to stop the hammering inside of her chest.

"Well, I have something I want to ask you, so I enlisted some help," he advised, nodding towards his friends. Then, jumping over the fence he stood in front her. "Of course, that one," pointing at Storm Cloud, "also insisted on helping." Glancing at the horse affectionately, she suddenly realized he had something hanging from his neck. Pointing, she looked at Mark, her expression baffled. "What is that?" she asked

"That," he said, as he reached over, untying the small box from his harness, "is a gift of sorts."

"Really?" she exclaimed. "For me? Mark, I don't underst—"

Suddenly, he opened the box, and there, nestled in a swath of white silk, rested the most incredibly beautiful ring she had ever seen. Kneeling, he held the precious gift towards her.

"Paige, I wasn't sure of how to do this, how to do it just right, but I couldn't help but hope that you would feel as I did, that it should include those that are closest to us." Glancing at their friends, she saw that Camilla and Maria were both crying, and she wasn't sure, but she thought that Adrian might just have shed a tear or two as well. Steve was grinning from ear to ear and when Paige looked back to Mark, she smiled. Encouraged, Mark continued.

"Paige, I want to do all of life with you by my side. Everything. No matter what it brings, I need you there. I want to fill our home with children who look like you and even add some dogs if Chloe agrees." As Paige laughed through her tears, he continued. "I only know," as he gently took her hand, "that you mean everything to me. I'm asking you," as he quickly glanced over at Storm Cloud, "we are asking you, please, will you marry me, Paige?"

For a moment, she closed her eyes, inhaling this moment. Absorbing into every cell of her body the way her heart felt beating in her ears, the goosebumps that traveled over her body, the tingling sensation that ran along her spine. Her breath was shallow from excitement, her legs weak from happiness. Then, opening her eyes, with every part of her singing a joyful song she quietly whispered. "Yes."

She felt him slide the ring onto her finger, then walked into his arms. After a few moments they were joined by their friends and it was so incredibly beautiful that it almost hurt, Paige thought, as she watched Steve pumping Mark's hand and Adrian hugging Maria. Camilla was by her side and the two friends didn't need words, simply stared into each other's eyes, a silent communion of friendship. Amid all the excitement Paige walked over to Storm Cloud. He raised his head, his eyes meeting hers, and in them she read his approval. The tears began anew as she once again recognized the extraordinary connection they had with him. Leaning over the fence he hung his head as she drew close to his ear.

"Thank you," she whispered. "I don't know how you managed to find me, but I will forever be grateful." Kissing his nose gently she turned, walking straight back into the arms of the man she had always belonged to.

Leaving Mark to go back to New York had been more difficult than Paige had anticipated, however, for the first few days she had been so busy that she found herself utterly exhausted at the end of each evening. They spoke at least three times a day and there was always a good night video chat. Still, now that she was an engaged woman with a wedding to plan, she found herself anxious to settle her affairs as soon as possible. Paul had been amazing, setting a remote schedule for her to conduct gallery business while also working out a travel itinerary that she would be able to handle. She had been able to sublet her apartment quickly which had been a great relief. At least fifty times a day she stared at the gorgeous ring on her finger, still trying to absorb that she had found her true love. Camilla was virtually chomping at the bit to start planning their wedding. A week after her return they sat comfortably in Paige's apartment, sipping hot chocolate, the atmosphere warm and cozy. Chloe, as usual, was curled up on Camilla's lap. Smiling over the rim of her cup Paige took a sip of the hot brew, then, placing it down, leaned back into the couch, wrapping her favorite blanket tightly around her. The weather was still freezing, and snow was predicted despite being close to the end of February.

"Where will you have the wedding?" Camilla asked, pulling her blanket up as well, momentarily causing Chloe to meow in protest.

"Oh, I have no idea really. Mark and I never got that far but I really don't care. Just as long as we get married," she finished dreamily, staring down at her ring.

Laughing, Camilla shook her head.

"Well, I hope you have a huge New York gala but I suspect," she continued mischievously, "that your fiancé may want something a little less glitzy."

Nodding, Paige once again picked up her drink, taking another sip before answering, picturing herself walking towards him.

"Agreed. I don't see him wanting anything too big," she replied, her voice thoughtful. "He loves the ranch so very much and I do as well. It would be a beautiful place to get married," she finished, her voice soft with happiness.

Observing her friend's contentment, Camilla smiled.

"You deserve this, my friend," she said, "and Mark is the best. I could never just give you to anyone who didn't deserve you," she finished, her eyes bright with unshed tears.

"You're going to make me cry," Paige exclaimed just as her phone vibrated. Glancing down she saw that it was Steve. Confused, she looked over at Camilla.

"That's strange," she said, a sudden sense of foreboding sweeping through her. Picking it up she placed it on speaker. "Hi Steve," she answered, her voice questioning.

"Paige," he began, his voice urgent. "I'm sorry to call so late. I'm so sorry Paige, but it's Mark." Suddenly, everything in her was on high alert, a burst of adrenaline coursing through her at breakneck speed. She felt hot and freezing at the same time, a bolt of fear racing down her spine. Throwing the blanket from her, she sat forward, gripping the phone so tightly her knuckles turned white.

"What happened?" she gulped, barely able to breathe.

"There was an accident. He was on his way back to the ranch with supplies. The weather has been terrible here and well, it was an oncoming car, Paige. It lost control and hit Mark's truck."

"Where is he?" she demanded.

"He's at the hospital here in Helena but Paige, it's bad," he finished, his voice choking.

Camilla bent near Paige, her hand resting on her shoulder.

"I'm on the way," she replied. "I will be on the first flight out."

"Paige, wait," he interrupted, "I think you should kn—"

"I don't need to know anything else Steve," she bit out, her expression hard. "Whatever it is, we will get through it together. I know Mark. I know him." Disconnecting the phone, she flung it onto the couch, then standing she observed Camilla's distress, tears coursing down her friend's cheeks.

"Stop crying, Camilla," Paige said firmly, making her way to her bedroom to pack. "You don't need to cry because Mark will be fine. I just know it." Wiping away her tears impatiently, Camilla watched her friend hurriedly call to get the next flight out, then quickly pack. She marveled at her calm determination, silently sending ending up a fervent plea that her friend was right.

CHAPTER 20

PAIGE RAGED AGAINST EVERY MINUTE, EVERY HOUR IT TOOK FOR her to get to Mark's side but finally she was walking into his room. Seeing him she stopped, then placed her hand on the wall to keep herself from sliding to the floor. He lay with a myriad of large machines surrounding him, their mechanical whispers the only sounds in the room. She made her way unsteadily towards him. His eyes were closed as she leaned down to kiss his forehead. Taking his hand, she rubbed his palm, willing him to wake up. After a few moments his eyes fluttered open. His smile pierced her heart. Paige had already spoken with his team of physicians and while they agreed he would survive, they felt it was highly likely that he would never walk again. Paige didn't agree. "He will walk again, she had insisted. You don't know him the way I do. I know he will."

His voice when he spoke was weak, and Paige had to lean in to hear him.

"You smell good," he said, causing a bubble of laughter to escape her lips.

"How do you feel?" she asked, trying not to sound anxious.

"Hmmm, well, kind of like I got hit by a truck," he answered, "which, from what I understand, is what actually happened."

Sitting in the chair by his bed, she squeezed his hand tightly.

"I'm so grateful you are here, and you are going to be fine," she whispered, giving in finally to the tears that now freely ran down her cheeks. "I love you so very much, Mark. I won't do this life without you so hurry up and get better."

Shaking his head, his expression was suddenly serious.

"I know they told you about my condition Paige. I won't ask you to spend your life with a man who cannot walk. I will not do that to you. You should know that now. In fact," he continued, his voice determined, "I believe we should end the engagement entirely."

Her expression incredulous, Paige sat backwards in the chair, his words like a physical blow.

"Have you lost your mind entirely, Mark Richards?" she barked, a flush of anger spreading from her chest to her face. "End the engagement? I think not," she spit out, pointing her finger at him. "I love you more than I can ever express, more than myself, more than— well, more than everything," she sputtered, unable to stem the hysteria that was now creeping into her voice. "We are not ending a thing! In fact, we will be starting a thing, a thing called our life together! You will marry me; Mr. Richards and it's going to be soon! Actually," she bellowed, shooting up from her chair and leaning over his bed, her voice ricocheting from the ceiling and walls, "it will be as soon as your incredibly sexy self is discharged from this very dreary hospital!"

As she stood there, her chest heaving, eyes spitting daggers of frustration towards him, Mark was reminded of a story his mother once read to him of a warrior princess who had been very brave and had saved all her people from a terrible giant who had been terrorizing them. The people had not thought that such a small woman could slay such a beast, but she had. Because she believed that she could. Watching her now, a sense of relief washed through him. She was terrifying, but she had faith. Mark had been petrified that she would take the ring off and simply walk away, yet he felt he had to give her the choice. Seeing her now, like this, he realized how incredibly fortunate he was to have this woman by his side. Suddenly, Paige realized that Mark was grinning at her, then he began to laugh, wincing slightly at the pain.

"You're laughing?" she accused him, still seething with anger. Crooking his finger at her, she slowly came closer, then, grabbing her arm, he pulled her down, kissing her with every bit of love he had. When she finally came up for air, she smiled at him warmly. Calm now, except for the ridiculous level of passion he had instantly awakened in her body with that kiss, she sat, folding her hands in her lap demurely.

"That's what I thought," she said, nodding her head firmly. "Now, let's talk about the wedding, Mr. Richards. We have so much to plan."

~

ON A GLORIOUS DAY IN APRIL, STEVE ROLLED HIS FRIEND'S wheelchair to the stable entrance, turning him so that he faced the back of the house. Once he had him settled in the right position, he smiled over at Camilla, adding a slow wink. Blushing furiously, Camilla quickly glanced away. Present were a handful of their closest friends and family and of course, Storm Cloud, who stood majestically, his gaze, too, on the large double doors. Soon, they opened, and Mark caught his breath when she finally emerged. Paul grasped Paige's elbow gently as they made their way slowly down the path, her gown trailing behind her. Simple but elegant, it was exactly what Mark envisioned his bride would wear. Her hair, entwined with wildflowers, hung loosely, blowing gently from the mountain breeze. He had been working hard in hopes he would be able to walk by the wedding, but he soon realized that it would be quite some time before that would happen. Finally, she was before him, and he watched as Paul gently kissed her cheek before going to stand beside Steve. He took her hand and read in her loving gaze all that he would ever need to know. Their vows were the truest words they had ever spoken, and soon they were one as they both knew they would always be.

Then, she took her husband's wheelchair and turned, headed towards the fence. Storm Cloud stood for a moment, simply observing them both, as Paige held her husband's hand. Then, stepping forward, he lowered his majestic head, rubbing his nose along Mark's jaw gently. Paige could see the love as Mark looked into his eyes. A moment later he turned towards Paige. When he didn't approach her, she felt confused. Then, suddenly, he backed up. Tossing his head several times, he carefully folded his leg, slowly going down in a bow. Stunned, all she could do was squeeze Mark's hand, tears running unchecked down her cheeks. Then, standing once again, he walked towards her, seeking her gaze. His love was evident, his acceptance of her a gift freely given. She smiled then, her love for this man and this beast filling her heart to overflowing.

EPILOGUE

She heard the screen door open and turned, smiling as she observed Maria make her way out. Paige could see the flour residue on her apron, a sure sign that her famous apple pie would be on the menu for dessert. At the thought, she felt her stomach turn, something it had been doing with increased regularity lately.

"Are you sure you don't want anything to drink?" Maria asked, making herself comfortable in the rocker beside her.

"I'm fine but thank you for asking." Nodding, she turned her attention to the front lawn.

"I don't know how those two can run around like that in this heat," Maria said, shaking her head. Laughing, Paige nodded her agreement.

"Well, I'm about to call them back in to clean up for dinner," she announced, and you know I'm going to get grief when I do."

Turning her attention back to her husband, Paige decided to give them a few more minutes, content to watch them play.

Mark carried their three-year-old son James, named after Mark's father, high on his shoulders as he jogged over to the fence line. She watched as Storm Cloud, along with his new foal made their way over to them, her son's excited laughter carrying over the warm summer evening. A sigh of contentment passed her lips as she drank in the extraordinary beauty that was her life.

"Maria," she spoke, her eyes brimming with tears of happiness, "you may want to bring Mark a small drink of whiskey with his pie tonight."

"Oh, why is that?" she asked, curious. Mark only drank on special occasions.

"Well," she replied as she stood to go gather her family, it looks like we will need nursery number two soon, a mischievous grin playing across her features as she placed her hand protectively across her abdomen. "He did say he wanted to fill our home with children."

Smiling, she made her way down the steps, her dogs Lilah and Boss right beside her. Breathing deeply, she walked barefoot across the soft grass, where everything in the world that she loved waited for her, arms wide open.

MEGAN'S CHOICE

We hope that you enjoyed this release from 5 Prince Publishing. The following is an excerpt from Darci Garcia's, Megan's Choice.

CHAPTER 1

MEGAN SLID HER UPPER TORSO SLIGHTLY FORWARD, SHIMMYING AS she worked herself further under the bed, her cheek skimming along the hardwood floor. Flipping back an errant blonde strand, she finally spied her prey, just out of reach. Stretching out her arm, fingers fully extended, she was mere millimeters away.

"Are you kidding me?" she mumbled, blowing a ball of dust out of the way. Dark eyes stared back from a broad, black muzzle sprouting fuzzy white patches. The flat black nose, surrounded by deep folds only added character to the obstinate disposition of its owner.

"Lucy, I mean it," Megan hissed, "come out right now." The muzzle in question belonged to Megan's Boston terrier. Currently, Lucy was holding Megan's favorite slingback shoe hostage, something she tended to do. It now dangled precariously between her large pink jowls.

"Want a cookie?" she asked, desperately. She hated to reward bad behavior with a treat but, let's face it, she thought, everyone does it. A blink of bright expressive eyes marked her reaction, as slobber slowly rolled off the destroyed shoe onto the floor.

Scooting back out, Megan stood, making a mental note to clean under the bed as she brushed the dirt off her shirt.

Entering her small kitchen, she grabbed one of Lucy's favorite snacks, then rushing back, knelt, placing the dog biscuit just past the edge of the bed. Leaning back on her heels, Megan waited. Predictably, within just a few seconds she heard a rustling sound along with the tap-tap of nails as Lucy made her way towards her treat. Peeking her head out, she gazed longingly at her bribe, her eyes darting between the prize and Megan's face. Placing her hand out, Megan simply stared at Lucy until finally, the mangled shoe slid from her jaws. Springing forward, she joyfully grabbed the treat, her hind end swaying happily as she made her way to her soft bed to savor the spoils. Sighing loudly, Megan observed the destroyed shoe, one of her favorites. They weren't too high or too low, she reflected sadly. Just the perfect in-between. Grasping it gingerly to avoid most of the saliva, she carried it to the kitchen trash, and giving it one last regretful glance, she tossed it in. Checking her watch, she hurried to find an alternate pair from her now depleted shoe rack. Glancing over her shoulder as she made her way back to her bedroom, she observed Lucy happily chomping away, the victor with her spoils. Smiling, Megan shook her head slightly, revisiting in her mind the day she had found her unruly dog.

It had been raining heavily, a gloomy afternoon in the quaint city of Bath, a small town located in Maine, just thirty minutes outside of Portland. Megan had been staring out the large window of her flower shop, contemplating the dismal day. On a whim she decided to close early. It had been busy, despite the weather, with excellent sales so she didn't feel too guilty calling it a day.

Megan had been saving since starting her first job working concessions at a movie theatre, even managing to get her business degree with no student loans. Working two jobs and studying had been the hardest thing she had ever done but ultimately, she had graduated, spending the next five years managing various businesses in preparation for opening her own store. Driven by her love of nature as well as a fierce desire to be the master of her destiny, she was finally able to open her flower shop. A bonus was its convenient location to an apartment complex within walking distance where she was able to rent while saving to buy her own home. Grabbing her umbrella, Megan had decided to brave the rain and head out. As she began hurrying down the sidewalk, she observed something black up ahead, huddled against the wall of another storefront. Blinking against the drops in her eyes, Megan could see it was a small dog, completely soaked, shivering and emaciated. As she approached, the exhausted creature looked at her, eyes sunken, brimming with pain and suffering. Raw empathy coursed through Megan. With no thought to the consequences, she knelt, placing her hand gently on top of its shaking head.

"You poor thing," she murmured, as she had leaned forward to better inspect the fragile creature. On closer examination, Megan could see it was a female. How could anyone abandon an innocent animal, she wondered, anger coursing through her.

"Well little one," she whispered softly as she carefully gathered the dog up, "it looks like it's you and me from now on." When their eyes met, Megan knew immediately that they were meant for each other. She had posted flyers in case the bedraggled puppy had belonged to someone who had simply lost the tiny canine, but no one came forward to claim her. Finally, Megan truly knew that the precious stray was home forever and decided, after some consideration, to name the pup, Lucy.

"I think it suits you," Megan told Lucy one evening, as the two snuggled on the couch. "Small, pretty and compact." They had settled in happily with each other and soon Megan couldn't remember a time that her hellion canine had not been a part of her life. Lucy even went to work with Megan every day, acquiring many adoring fans amongst the flower shop's clientele.

The only downside had turned out to be the effect on Megan's love life.

There had been several boyfriends, but Lucy had made it quite clear that she didn't like any of them. In fact, they were sure to be the recipient of her special brand of bullying that included a determined glare, a threatening growl and for added effect, she would occasionally even bare her teeth. Ultimately, her guest would make a hasty retreat. Their behavior was completely understandable, however, there was the hopelessly romantic part of her that felt the right man could win her self-charged protector over.

If not, I will just remain single, she thought, or maybe start adding some cats? Shaking her head, she dismissed the idea. Too soon, she assured herself. Still, Megan was fine with being unattached. At just twenty-eight she was in no hurry for marriage. One day she would like to find love, the kind that ended in a genuine happily ever after, yet there was a part of her that wasn't entirely sure she would recognize if it even did happen. So far no one had ever given her the shivers. She had read about that once in a particularly steamy romance novel and it had stuck with her. Still, she thought, I may not be deliriously happy, but I am reasonably content.

Her parents, Elizabeth and Douglas Cunningham, lived close by as did her younger sister Lindsey, and they visited each other often. Lindsey would spend occasional nights over, the two women frequently lying awake in bed talking and giggling into the wee hours with Lucy nestled between them, snoring softly. Megan's best friend Gabby was also a regular visitor, although, having married last year they didn't see each other as much as they used to. Megan had found the announcement of Gabby's engagement bittersweet. She knew that although they would always be close, things would change, and Megan couldn't help but feel sorrowful at the loss of that special time in their lives. Feeling a nudge on the small of her back, Megan turned from her kneeling position in front of her closet. Lucy stood; her leash clenched in her mouth.

"Ok," Megan laughed. Choosing a pair of flats, she stood up. "I know, I know, it's time to go." Sliding into her shoes, she quickly snapped on Lucy's leash. Grabbing her purse along with Lucy's dog bag off the counter, they headed out. Stepping into the hallway, she marveled once again at the choice of carpeting that ran the length of the long corridor. Its spiral circles in bright oranges and deep blue always made her a little dizzy. As Megan turned to make her way to the elevator, she noticed activity several doors down. Men wearing polo shirts that read *We Move Everything* were busy carrying boxes into the empty apartment. Must be a new neighbor moving in, she thought. Suddenly, Lucy began pulling on her leash while Megan kept trying to gently wrest her back, however, she seemed unusually fascinated by the movers.

"Lucy, stop," Megan commanded. Normally the dog trotted directly to the elevator, never interested in any of the residents, even when they tried to pet her. Suddenly, Megan felt the leash go lax, then watched as it dropped away from the harness. She realized too late that she had not secured it properly. Sensing she was free, Lucy sprang forward.

"Lucy no," Megan scolded, chasing her down the hallway. With a sinking sensation, she watched as her disobedient dog veered sharply right, into the empty unit. Panicked, Megan reached the open door. Just as she was about to enter, she crashed headlong into a chest. A very large, very male chest. Immediately a strong hand grasped her shoulder, helping to steady her as she rocked back from the impact. Breathless, she looked up. The stranger's eyes were startling, an icy blue mixed with slate. Extraordinary, she thought, fascinated by their hue.

"Are you ok?" the man asked, his brow furrowed in concern.

"What?" Megan stuttered, staring up at him, completely unable to form a cohesive thought. This is exactly why you're still single, she thought, still mute. Just then Lucy began barking furiously. Horrified, Megan observed her errant dog run deliriously over the stranger's very expensive leather couch. Her tongue hung almost to her feet as she trailed drool joyously. The man had turned away from her, staring incredulously.

"Is that your dog?" he asked without turning.

"That dog?" Megan squeaked. "No. I mean yes, yes of course she is," then, pushing past the stranger, Megan ran towards Lucy who wasn't the least bit concerned by the murderous look on Megan's face. Instead, she proceeded to jump from the couch to a large, overstuffed chair. There, Lucy grabbed a bright yellow throw pillow that had been resting on the arm, simultaneously chewing and tossing it from side to side. Horrified, Megan stood rooted as her mind tried to absorb the sheer lunacy of this moment.

"Please drop the pillow, please, please," she repeated, under her breath. By now, Megan was praying for the floor to open up and swallow her whole. That or instant death. Either would work, she thought, practically panting with embarrassment. Her silk shirt had slipped out of her waistband, and when she had lunged for Lucy, she lost a shoe. They were her slightly too big ones that she had been forced to wear due to her devil canine. By now, Megan was sweating profusely, her distress hovering somewhere in the acute range. I must look simply stunning, she thought hysterically, still very much aware of the gorgeous male watching the destruction of his personal property unfold. Grabbing the pillow, Megan pulled it, still attached to Lucy, towards her. Just as her finger was about to slide under the collar bearing the name of that worthless puppy training school, she heard a terrible ripping sound, accompanied by a cloud of exploding white feathers. Excited, Lucy let go of the pillow, jumping to the floor as she chased the floating white creatures in circles. Both Megan and Lucy were covered in the white plumage, small pieces of yellow fabric mixed in. Megan watched in shocked fascination as the carnage floated onto the stranger's floor, her stomach sinking to somewhere under her feet.

Just as Megan was about to begin the chase again, Lucy was swept off the floor into the arms of the blue-eyed man. Immediately, she slowed her panting, quickly dragging her dangling tongue back into her mouth, her eyes fixed adoringly on him. Lucy appeared to be listening intently, her head cocked slightly, large ears standing straight up, as the stranger murmured sweet nothings to her. Megan instantly started forward to take her when Lucy licked his face once, then proceeded to rest her quill-strewn head in the crook of his neck. Dumbfounded, Megan could only stare. Lucy had never exhibited such immediate fondness for anyone else, not even her sister, Lindsey or her parents who doted on her. Yet clearly, she felt something special for this man. Well, Megan thought, not only was she a shoe carnivore, she was clearly also a traitor.

Walking forward, Megan was encouraged by the stranger's smile. He had flawlessly straight, white teeth and Megan couldn't help but notice the tiny crow's feet by his almond shaped eyes, that had no doubt been placed ever so perfectly, by his own personal angel on high. His hair was kohl black, smoothed back and very thick. Upon closer inspection she observed, as well, his commanding bone structure framed by a square, even brow. His nose ended in a blunt plane rather than a point which only enhanced his rugged good looks. Noting how gently he held Lucy, something inside of Megan warmed.

"I cannot apologize enough—" she began, but the dog whisperer interrupted.

"I hated that pillow anyway," he replied laughingly. "I will assume that this beauty is Lucy. It was the name you were yelling," he finished, clearly amused.

"The one and only," Megan affirmed, still working through ten levels of embarrassment. She could feel the sweat on her brow but refused to further humiliate herself by attempting to wipe it with the sleeve of her silk blouse, "Mutilator of shoes and —at the risk of getting too personal—the queen of flatulence."

Too much information, she thought, wincing inwardly. Reaching forward, Megan took Lucy from the man, placing her gently on the floor as she reattached her leash. Glancing around at the chaos, Megan spied her shoe. Attempting to maintain what shreds of dignity remained, she limped majestically over to retrieve it. Sliding it on, she then tucked in her shirt. Finally dressed, she reached out her hand.

"I'm Megan Cunningham," she announced, "I live a few doors down, which may or may not cause you to reconsider your choice of apartment complex."

Laughing, he shook her hand firmly. "Brice Castillo," he offered, his eyes intense as they moved over her. Megan felt her heart begin to beat not so much faster but harder, the sensation leaving her slightly breathless. Megan allowed herself a leisurely moment to examine the male specimen before her. He was very tall, possibly more than six feet, she observed. His white shirt hugged his shoulders and arms, and Megan could see the muscles that flexed when he moved. His jeans, slightly faded, stretched over thighs that were thick and powerful. He was barefoot, which for some strange reason, caused Megan's respirations to tick up a few notches. It had not escaped her notice—because she purposely looked—that his left hand was devoid of a wedding ring. Suddenly feeling magnanimous, she smiled down at Lucy warmly, her eyes slowly widening in horror when she realized there was a small puddle forming around her. Heart plummeting, she closed her eyes briefly, silently shaking her fist at the fates.

"Lucy, no!" Megan cried. Glancing down, Brice quickly grabbed a roll of paper towels resting on the kitchen counter and before Megan could help, he bent, quickly wiping the floor himself.

"That's it," Megan stated, her face beet red, "we are leaving before she destroys something else. Again, I am so sorry for everything." Glancing down at Lucy's angelic face, she continued, "I have no idea what has gotten into her. I mean she's usually so good, and well, I'm just really sorry…" she finished breathlessly, furiously brushing feathers off her shirt. Waving away her apology, Brice threw the wet towels away and after quickly rinsing his hands, followed Megan and Lucy as they made their way to the door. Stepping into the hall, Megan turned, placing her hand out once again.

"Please, at least let me replace your pillow," Megan began, but Brice shook his head.

"That won't be necessary," he assured her, sending Lucy a gentle smile. "It was wonderful to meet you both and I certainly hope we see each other again." Bending, he patted Lucy's head as she looked up at him rapturously. Good grief, Megan thought, she is really laying it on thick. "Maybe after the rest of my furniture arrives?"

Flustered, Megan replied. "Yes, I would like that. I'm just down the hall in unit B."

Taking a deep breath, she gave a half wave as she turned, heading once more towards the elevator, mentally scolding herself for her awkwardness. He probably thinks I'm a lunatic, she thought, resisting the urge to turn around. Megan could feel his eyes on her back and was relieved when she finally heard his door close. That went well, she thought, wiping sweat from her forehead. Welcome to the neighborhood.

PLEASE RATE AND REVIEW

We hope you enjoyed *Paige and the Reluctant Artist* by Darci Garcia. If you did, we would ask that you please rate and review this title. Every review helps our authors.

Rate and Review: Paige and the Reluctant Artist

MEET THE AUTHOR

Darci Garcia is a Contemporary Romance Writer who calls sunny Florida home. Along with a child or two, an extremely patient husband and five rescue dogs, her days are filled with a great deal of chaos, but even more love as she lives out her own happily ever after.

185